AF304829

SHACKLE *the* STORM

SHACKLE the STORM

A Collection of *Thrilling Tales*

SHAILENDRA SRIVASTAVA

RUPA

Published by
Rupa Publications India Pvt. Ltd 2024
7/16, Ansari Road, Daryaganj
New Delhi 110002

Sales Centres:
Bengaluru Chennai Hyderabad
Jaipur Kathmandu Kolkata
Mumbai Prayagraj

P-ISBN: 978-93-5702-681-9
E-ISBN: 978-93-5702-824-0

First impression 2024

10 9 8 7 6 5 4 3 2 1

The moral right of the author has been asserted.

Printed in India

Contents

Introduction

Shackle the Storm is a collection of 14 gripping stories that emerge from personal experiences, revealing a world of killers, scammers, rapists, terrorists, Maoists, rioters, kidnappers and underworld criminals. These are not mere works of fiction but true accounts of harrowing events that unfolded before me and my colleagues in the police force.

Inspired by real-life crimes, these captivating narratives offer readers an engaging and insightful exploration of crime investigations and the challenges of maintaining public order. With each story, readers are drawn deeper into the relentless pursuit of justice, where lives hang in the balance and the line between order and chaos becomes increasingly thin.

Within the pages of this book you will encounter the chilling account of two young girls who met the same tragic end, leaving a community engulfed in mystery. Their story serves as a haunting reminder of the dangers lurking in our midst. You will also find tales of intricate kidnapping plots for hefty ransoms, brutal blasts triggered by Maoists to eliminate law enforcement officers, the cold-blooded murder of a young girl by one of her own family members, wrongful imprisonment and the allegation of gang rape in a vehicle, among others. With scenes of decapitated bodies, blood flowing within temple premises and corpses with severed heels, these tales will send shivers down your spine.

Each crime scene bore the chilling imprint of malevolent forces and enigmatic predators, erasing any trace of evidence. As the pieces of these puzzles grew more perplexing with each revelation and exposed a labyrinth of deception deeply entrenched within the community, through meticulous investigations, we managed to unveil the truth every time.

You will encounter a cast of characters driven by greed, lust, power and passion in these narratives. From notorious gangsters like Dawood Ibrahim to ordinary individuals thrust into extraordinary circumstances, each character is bound by their own motivations and desires.

As law enforcement officers, we frequently face daunting challenges, from quelling communal violence to unravelling complex criminal conspiracies. Our relentless pursuit of justice often leads us into perilous situations, where we must navigate dense forests and treacherous terrains, and confront the notorious characters head-on to hold them accountable for their heinous crimes.

Through these pages, I have celebrated the bravery, intelligence and resolute commitment to justice demonstrated by men and women in uniform. Unlike fictional detectives like James Bond or Hercule Poirot, the protagonists in these stories are police officers who fearlessly risk their lives to save victims and colleagues amidst billowing smoke and impenetrable darkness. Their commitment to justice serves as an inspiration to us all.

While writing this book, I strived to strike a balance between authenticity and honouring the privacy and reputation of the individuals involved. It is important to note that although the events and circumstances described in these tales are rooted in reality, the names, places and specific identifying details of the accused, victims and other relevant parties have been altered to safeguard their identities while simultaneously upholding ethical standards. This alteration of elements aims to create a work of non-fiction that maintains the integrity of the original stories while respecting the rights and dignity of those involved. Any resemblance to actual persons, living or deceased, is purely coincidental. However, throughout the book, I have tried my best to recognize and praise the dedicated efforts and commitment of the investigating police officers. Therefore, their actual names have been retained as a tribute to their invaluable contributions in the pursuit of justice.

My aim in sharing these tales is to reaffirm the age-old adage that truth always prevails. These stories are more than just ink on paper; they are a testament to the unyielding human spirit and the enduring pursuit of truth.

Satyameva Jayate

1

The Lucky Baton

Separated by time yet united by a haunting darkness, two young girls, brimming with innocence and vitality, found their lives abruptly cut short. In a dramatic turn of events, the investigation yielded results, revealing the perpetrator and stripping away the carefully masterminded deceitful facade.

On a lazy spring afternoon, I found myself reclining on a couch in my study, captivated by the melodic warbles of the winged pipers emanating from my garden. As I scanned the room, my eyes settled upon a baton nestled in a cosy nook against the wall. This baton held special significance for me, a memento presented by my friend and fellow trainee, Mr Jaffar Sait, during our time at the National Police Academy. Acquired during our Indian Army attachment in Kashmir, it had been crafted by a talented Kashmiri girl and serves as a constant reminder of the cherished moments spent with my friend.

Each time my gaze falls upon this baton, a multitude of memories of past investigations come rushing back. I believe that it possesses some power that has helped me solve even the most intricate cases. In addition to being visually appealing, it seems to be the key to my success in capturing numerous criminals. I would now like to recount one such case that I solved with the aid of this very baton.

After completing my training at the National Police Academy, I was assigned to the Madhya Pradesh cadre as an assistant superintendent of police in Ratlam district. In my quest for comprehensive experience, I willingly assumed duties at every level within the police force, from constable to superintendent of police (SP), within the district. Ratlam, known for its communal sensitivity, had become a haven for drug peddlers. After undergoing training in patrolling and investigation, I was assigned to the motor transport and reserve police lines.

Subsequently, I had the opportunity to work alongside Deputy Superintendent of Police (DSP) [Headquarters] R.R. Patidar, a seasoned and highly competent officer who imparted invaluable knowledge about various aspects of policing. He was also in charge of the Bilpank and Namli police stations. Accompanying the deputy superintendent, I visited these police stations, engaging with the staff and familiarizing myself with their operations. Eventually, I was posted at Namli police station as an under-training station house officer.

One morning, a call from the SP of Ratlam alerted me to a grim incident in Semliya village. A 13-year-old girl had been killed, and he assigned the case to me for investigation. Accompanied by an assistant, I rushed to the police station on a motorbike. Upon arrival, I learnt that the police station staff had already gone to Semliya village to initiate the investigation. The village where the incident had occurred was approximately 4 km from Namli.

According to the information gathered, the perpetrator had brutally killed a minor girl, callously discarding her body in a sack near a drain in an isolated area of the village. The girl, who had left her home the previous day to sell radish roots, never returned. As night fell, her parents and fellow villagers initiated a search that lasted until dawn. The discovery of her lifeless body revealed that the perpetrator had not only strangled her but also mutilated her by severing her heels to extract the silver anklets she had been wearing.

As we delved into the case, it came to our attention that a similar incident had occurred seven years earlier. In that case too, the perpetrator had followed the same pattern of violating and strangling a girl before removing her anklets by severing her heels. The body of the previous victim had also been discarded on the outskirts of the village. Even after seven years, the police had failed to discover any substantial leads and the case had been closed. The incident ignited intense anger among the villagers. They expressed deep resentment by shuttering their shops in both Semliya and Namli, protesting the perceived failure of the police to apprehend the culprit.

When we reached the site where the second girl's body was discovered, an eerie silence enveloped us. Many villagers had gathered around, their anger palpable and their lack of trust in the police understandable. They believed that the policemen had merely arrived to complete formalities and that the issue would be buried within a day or two, allowing the murderer to escape justice again. Despite my efforts to reassure the influential individuals of the village, promising to apprehend the culprit and bring them to justice, my words seemed to fall on deaf ears.

While examining the girl's body, I noticed a distinctive blue mark around her neck, which indicated strangulation. Furthermore, it became evident that the killer had severed her heels before extracting the anklets. Drawing on my background as a police officer with knowledge of forensic science, I deduced that the victim had been murdered several hours earlier. Consequently, the body had already undergone rigor mortis, making it impossible to remove the anklets without severing the heels.

To gather further evidence, we called in a female doctor to examine the body. Following her thorough examination, she concluded, 'The criminal violated her before ending her life.' We then sent the body for a post-mortem examination; once the necessary formalities were completed, we handed the body over to the grieving relatives for the last rites. Given her tender age, the girl's mortal remains were laid to rest.* I stood as a witness at the burial site, acutely aware of the profound anguish experienced by her family and the villagers. Subsequently, we returned to the police station, the journey shrouded in solemn silence.

Upon our return, I delved into the case file related to a similar incident that had occurred seven years ago. We meticulously

---

*It is the village custom for minors to be buried rather than cremated.

studied the case and made notes of pertinent facts and details. Engaging in extensive brainstorming sessions, we explored various possibilities and lines of further investigation. As my team and I examined each page of the case file, it became increasingly apparent that the present incident mirrored the one from seven years ago. A realization dawned upon me: the same individual may be responsible for both murders.

⤜⤛

My team and I gathered all available information about the 13-year-old girl. We discovered that she used to sell vegetables from a basket and had left her house with it. When she failed to return home, she was reported missing. Our search for the culprit led us to search every house in the village. However, finding the proverbial needle in a haystack proved to be an arduous task. Despite our efforts, the crucial break we sought remained elusive. As dusk settled in, the empty, dusty roads and chorus of buzzing cicadas intensified the approaching darkness, enveloping the village in an eerie silence. We decided to spend the night in the hamlet and then resumed our house-to-house search at daybreak. Our team cordoned off the area around the victim's house in the village, as well as the neighbouring region where the body was found, closely monitoring the villagers' activities.

Exhaustion plagued our team and I sought to uplift my colleagues' spirits by reassuring them: 'Do not despair. We will soon apprehend the murderer. Nothing can deter us.' My sole objective was to capture the perpetrator and ensure they faced the consequences. On the other hand, resentment among the villagers continued to deepen; they remained doubtful of our capabilities, perceiving me, a youthful-looking sub-inspector (SI), as lacking the necessary expertise to crack the case.

My thoughts drifted back to the spot where the girl was last seen. 'Let us return to the spot from where the girl went missing,' I suggested. We discovered a thatched house near the location. Its owner, a conscientious citizen, had played an active role in rallying the villagers for the search throughout the night. He cooperated with the police and even allowed us to search his house.

I carried the lucky baton with me as we searched the two-room thatched house. Frustrated by the lack of evidence, I struck a wall of the house with my baton. To my astonishment, the swift strike of my baton caused a basket to plummet to the floor, revealing a few radish leaves clinging to it. Recalling what the girl's mother had shared, I presented the basket to her at her residence. Tears welled up in her eyes as she confirmed, 'My daughter used this hamper to sell vegetables.'

The house owner's gentle appearance made it hard to fathom that he could have committed such a crime. Seemingly anticipating the troubles that lay ahead, he had joined the villagers in their search for the girl and fully cooperated with the police, leaving no room for doubt regarding his innocence. His composed demeanour shocked us all.

'I raped and murdered the minor girl seven years ago, before I was married. After my marriage, my wife became an accomplice to the second crime,' he confessed.

'My wife coveted the silver anklets that the girl was wearing, whereas I desired a physical relationship with her. When the girl passed by our house, I lured her inside. My wife held her from behind while I raped her. Subsequently, we both strangled her,' he revealed.

Once the couple had murdered the girl, they hid her body inside the house. When the villagers initiated a fervent search for the missing girl, the perpetrator, to avoid drawing attention to him, joined in the search efforts. By the time he returned home, the girl's body had stiffened, making it incredibly difficult to remove the anklets.

'I severed her heels and retrieved the anklets. We then placed her body in a sack and left it near the drain,' he admitted.

The shared destiny of both young girls had befallen them. We were momentarily stunned by the criminal's confession, grappling with the heinous acts he had committed.

I immediately informed the SP about the breakthrough and he commended us for solving both cases. Our actions not only restored the villagers' faith in the police department but also reignited respect for our profession. This case marked the first successful investigation in my career as a police officer, providing me with a profound sense of satisfaction. However, the brutal murders of two innocent girls cast a grave shadow over my joy of having solved the case. I could empathize with the profound anguish experienced by their family members.

Throughout my investigative journey, I have carried the lucky baton with me: it has been a divine beacon guiding me through the darkness. Every time I look at it, the chilling incidents of Semliya village in Namli and many other cases resurface in my mind. These memories will always remain with me, serving as a constant reminder of the horrors that humanity is capable of perpetrating.

2

The Unholy Sacrifice

Many criminals justify their actions by claiming they committed certain crimes in response to what they perceive as a divine command. Consequently, they may never express remorse for their deeds.

The days were getting shorter and evenings descended early as autumn approached. At that time, I was the subdivisional officer (SDO) of police, stationed in the Neemuch subdivision of Mandsaur district.

I was in my office, observing dusk settle over the rain-fed wooded land of Neemuch through the window, when a constable burst into the room. 'A girl has died accidentally in a temple near the police station,' he informed me.

Without hesitation, I mobilized my team and headed to the scene. It was customary for me to visit the scene of a serious crime to gain first-hand knowledge about the incident, a practice I never overlooked.

Upon reaching the temple, I found the girl's body lying face down before the idol of Goddess Kali, blood pooling around it. A sword lay nearby. Given the absence of a female constable at the police station, I attempted to examine the body on my own, only to be rendered speechless by what I discovered: her severed head lay on the temple floor as blood flowed from it like a small stream. With her body in my hands and her head on the ground, I was momentarily paralysed, confronted with a level of horror unlike any I had experienced before.

Her family members who were present there evaded my questions when I inquired about the incident. They insisted they were unaware of the circumstances that had led to her untimely demise. My instincts suggested they were withholding the truth, so I probed deeper. Under pressure, one of her family members finally revealed the truth.

Lalbag, the area where the incident had taken place, was marked by poverty, widespread superstition and a lack of education. Most of the people in this region belonged to the poor and weaker sections. Shyam Lal, the deceased girl's father, had gone to the Nimbahera area of Rajasthan in search of a livelihood, taking his family with him.

Shyam Lal's wife's cousin, Sanju, suffered from stomach pain and occasionally fainted. Shyam Lal and his family believed that only Saloni, his younger daughter and considered a blessed child of Goddess Kali, possessed the ability to cure Sanju. So Saloni was summoned back to Neemuch.

On the morning marking the commencement of the 10-day Ganesh festival, Sanju and Saloni secluded themselves in a temple within Shyam Lal's residence, fervently praying to Goddess Kali. Despite the concerned family members' persistent attempts to attract their attention, they refrained from opening the door or appearing for meals even after an extended period.

The door was finally opened by a child who was made to enter the room through a window. A horrifying sight awaited them in the room: Saloni was lying on her stomach and the floor was drenched in her blood. Sanju, whose body was also soaked in blood, lay unconscious beside her. Saloni was already dead by the time most of the villagers arrived at the scene.

When Sanju briefly regained consciousness, his family members asked what had happened to Saloni. He gave only one reply—that he had done nothing and that it all happened as per the goddess' intent. When a few villagers suggested informing the police, Sanju pleaded against it. Sanju further said that Saloni had told him she would come to life and that he should keep the temple door closed until it happened.

Sanju then explained what Saloni had told him: 'You must offer my head to Goddess Kali as it will cure you of stomach pain and bring prosperity to the family.'

Sanju stated that while he was unwilling to perform such an

act, Saloni remained resolute and instructed him to place her severed head near her neck believing that she would be revived. He went on to admit, 'As soon as she directed me, I cut off her head with the sword.'

The villagers believed what Sanju said and began waiting for her to come back to life. Several hours passed but Saloni did not rise from the dead, so one of the villagers finally decided to inform the police.

During the initial phase of the investigation, Saloni's family members were reluctant to divulge information. They concocted a story that Saloni had accidentally hurt herself while playing with a sword. What they were saying defied all logic: one cannot chop off their head while playing with a sword. Therefore, I continued the line of questioning the whole night, when finally, Saloni's uncle admitted that Sanju had decapitated her. Following this statement, we immediately arrested Sanju.

None of my team members had ever encountered such a horrifying sight. As dawn arrived, we were greeted by the drumbeats and sounds of conch shells from a nearby temple, heralding the arrival of the idols of Lord Ganesh in procession for immersion in a nearby waterbody. Lost in my thoughts about the young girl, I was startled when my driver broke the silence and said, 'Sir, it is morning now. Let's go home.'

Sanju remained seemingly unaffected—as if nothing had happened. Similarly, Saloni's parents did not hold any anger towards the perpetrator, interpreting the incident as a divine command. This incident made me contemplate the prevalence of superstition in many parts of our country. The people of Lalbag still believe that if they hadn't hastily opened the door, the girl would have miraculously come back to life.

3

. . . .

The Storm Peters Out

Singoli, a small town in Madhya Pradesh, became the focal point of unrest when a band of agitators torched a power substation. Their fury stemmed from enduring sleepless nights without electricity. As a newcomer to the area, I failed to grasp the depth of their anger and the political undercurrents fuelling their agitation. What followed was a nightmarish ordeal.

I was posted in Neemuch as an SDO of police in the late 1980s. My batchmate and an Indian Administrative Services (IAS) officer, Anil Jain, was the subdivisional magistrate (SDM). He was known not only for his fairness and impartiality but also for being well acquainted with the problems of the area. Consequently, he earned the respect of members of various political organizations and was equally favoured by the locals. On the second day of my posting, I had dinner with Jain at his residence, where he generously shared invaluable insights about the Neemuch subdivision and offered professional guidance.

At around 11 p.m., I was driving home from Jain's residence when I saw an elderly person walking on the road. I recognized him as someone I had met earlier at a peace committee meeting, where he had introduced himself as Thakur Sahab, a former legislator and a prominent figure of the political party that was then in the opposition. He had secured victory in the assembly elections twice as a candidate of this party.

I pulled over and asked him his destination. He told me that he was going home, which was 4 km away. Given his seniority, I requested him to sit in my vehicle in order to drop him off at his house. After much persuasion, he gave in. We reached his place within 10 minutes. During our journey, he asked me many questions about my qualifications, family members and reasons for becoming a police officer. He also mentioned the names of several senior police officers with whom he had good relations. As soon as I stopped my vehicle outside his house, he invited me in for a cup of tea. However, I politely declined due to the late hour, promising to visit another time. He commented that I was a good human being and wished me all the best for my future assignments.

He also said that I had not done the right thing by dropping him off at his home in my vehicle. When I asked him the reason for his comment, he said that while he was thankful to me, the ruling party would turn against me.

Thakur Sahab said, 'My rival is a legislator from this area. The member of Parliament (MP) is also from this place. Both belong to my rival political party.' He further said, 'Since you are a good person, I could not turn down your offer to drop me off at my house, but don't tell anyone.' We bid each other goodnight, and then I took a round of the city before finally reaching home at 12.30 a.m.

⤫

It was 3.30 a.m. when I suddenly woke up to the ringing of my phone. I picked up the call and identified the voice on the other side as Anil Jain's. He told me to get ready and that he was coming to my residence to pick me up because there was a big agitation in Singoli.

He also conveyed that he had already informed the collector about the situation and suggested that I dispatch a substantial police contingent to the scene. Additionally, he recommended mobilizing forces from Ratangarh and Jawad, the closest police stations to Singoli, to ensure adequate presence of policemen at the site upon our arrival. I quickly prepared to leave, accompanied by my gunman and driver, while simultaneously coordinating the movement of the forces through wireless communication.

I called Anil Bhatt, the town inspector (TI) of Neemuch, to my house. Meanwhile, Jain also reached my residence, and our group set out for the site of the agitation. Throughout the journey, I remained occupied with the wireless set, directing policemen to move towards Singoli and verifying whether the force had reached the spot. Furthermore, I informed the SP, the Thanedar (police station in-charge) and other officers of Singoli that Anil Jain and I would soon reach the spot.

Our team reached the epicentre of the agitation at 8 a.m., slightly later than anticipated, despite the location being only 120 km from Neemuch, due to the numerous potholes along the road. There was a curfew-like situation in the area. We reached the police station, where a few administrative officers were already present, and the tehsildar (revenue officer) narrated the incident to us. He said that there had been a blackout the previous night at Singoli and that it was a recurring incident. The frequent power failures had sparked anger among locals. In addition to being unable to maintain a consistent power supply, the electricity department officials were also rude to the people. Despite complaints to the Naib tehsildar (subordinate of a tehsildar) about the frequent power failures, he neither paid any attention to the issue nor did anything to address the grievances.

On one occasion, the villagers had mistreated an official, subjecting him to public humiliation by parading him around the town in torn clothes. Despite this, the official opted not to report the incident to higher authorities, and it was, as usual, overlooked. When the power went the night before, public anger spilt on to the streets. Members of the opposition party's youth wing gathered outside the electricity office, chanting slogans. The power substation in-charge locked his office and escaped through the back door, further intensifying the residents' frustration. Their anger stemmed from enduring sleepless nights due to the lack of electricity and the unresponsiveness of the authorities. This outrage escalated, prompting some residents to set fire to the power substation.

The area had gained notoriety for such incidents. The inability of the police and local administration to improve the situation only increased the frustration and led to potential misconduct. However, this time, provided with a sufficient police force, the authorities acted improperly, assaulting the agitators and seeking retribution for the previous incident involving the mistreatment of the revenue officer. This resulted in multiple arrests and the filing of four first information reports (FIRs).

Upon arriving in Singoli and assessing the situation, the SDM informed the collector about the details of the events over the phone. The collector instructed the authorities to arrest the culprits and transfer them to the Ratangarh police station. However, at the Ratangarh police station, both revenue and police officials behaved aggressively, settling old scores by verbally abusing and severely beating the agitators, resulting in unethical custodial violence. I was unaware of the events at the Ratangarh police station. In hindsight I realize that it was a significant lapse and mistake on the part of the police and administration.

⁓

Given that it was only my third day of posting in the area, I could not fully grasp the gravity of the rapidly unfolding situation. While the ruling party welcomed the action taken, suggesting that police officers across the state should adopt similar heavy-handed tactics in handling agitators, the opposition party saw it as an opportunity to capitalize on, launching a state-wide agitation. They vehemently opposed the incident and formed an inquiry team under the leadership of the then opposition leader in the assembly. The following day, the team arrived in Singoli. I remained there to restore normalcy, while Jain had returned to Neemuch to preside over a pre-scheduled revenue court. My working style was unfamiliar to everyone since I was new to the area. Consequently, rumours began circulating in the town, portraying me as an officer with a dubious past who was promoted and assigned as the SDO of police. I was depicted no differently from a typical antagonist in a Bollywood blockbuster—known for his fierce demeanour, heavy drinking and constant betel chewing.

The higher authorities in Bhopal bought into this fabricated portrayal of me. When the leader of the opposition arrived at the guest house in Singoli, I extended a warm welcome to him. As the position of the leader of the opposition is equal to that of a cabinet minister, we saluted him as per the protocol. I offered him tea and biscuits, and just as he started sipping his tea, his party workers paraded to the guest house in a procession. They chanted anti-police and anti-district administration slogans and directed abuses at me. They had made an effigy bearing my name and torched it before my eyes. Despite the distressing sight, I maintained my composure and resilience, fully aware of such challenges being part and parcel of my responsibilities within the police department.

The opposition leader asked, 'Who is Shailendra Srivastava against whom the agitators are using such derogatory words and whose effigy they are burning?'

I responded calmly, 'I'm the person the agitators are targeting because they think I'm responsible for all that is happening.'

He appeared surprised and expressed his belief in my character, acknowledging the possibility of misunderstandings. He calmed the agitators and accompanied them to the site, where I ensured ample security arrangements for him. After assessing the area and gathering inputs from the villagers, he returned to the guest house. Taking me aside, he reassured me, saying, 'I've comprehended the situation. Some members of our party caused disturbances for both the police and the administration. Even though the police and local authorities resorted to violence, I can see that you were not involved. Do not worry; nothing will happen to you.'

I felt a surge of relief upon hearing his words.

I was fortunate to serve in the police department during a time when political parties generally held favourable opinions about administrative officials and law enforcement officers. Since the aggrieved party belonged to the opposition, the agitators in Singoli were against me, whereas those from Mandsaur and Neemuch, with whom I had previously interacted, extended their support. Upon my return to Neemuch after four days, Thakur Sahab visited my office.

He said, 'We do not hold any personal grudge against you. Though you are a gentleman of integrity, as I have witnessed myself, we are leveraging your name to put pressure on the government. We are highlighting this issue due to its political significance and intend to initiate a protest against the police in general.' Thakur Sahab also revealed that the opposition party was likely to come into power in the next assembly election.

Thakur Sahab facilitated a phone conversation with a former legislator from Mandsaur, who corroborated this information. He emphasized that their intention was to target the ruling party and not me specifically, even though they would be using my name.

The blueprint for this state-wide agitation was under development. According to their scheme, three senior leaders were scheduled to commence a fast unto death in Singoli the following day. Similarly, three other leaders were planning a hunger strike against me in Neemuch. Additionally, three former chief ministers were preparing to initiate a fast unto death outside the current chief minister's residence in Bhopal, intending to submit a memorandum to him. The memorandum would demand action against me, suspension of the Singoli police station staff, the filing of criminal cases against the police officers and unconditional release of the agitators.

Furthermore, the president of the opposition party was scheduled to arrive in Neemuch to deliver a speech against me, accompanied by several other senior leaders of their party. They also intended to burn my effigy during the meeting. Subsequently, the party president would return to Bhopal the following day to deliver a memorandum to the chief minister and commence a fast unto death.

The ex-legislator also mentioned to me that the agitation would persist until my transfer from Neemuch.

As planned, the president of the opposition party arrived in Neemuch in the evening and delivered a speech to a large crowd. I organized all the security measures and installed barricades around the stage to prevent any unforeseen incidents.

After the meeting, the president left for Singoli, where he met the family members of those who were detained in Ratangarh police station. He then left for Bhopal the next morning, where he, along with two former chief ministers met the chief minister, and handed the memorandum to him. Subsequently, they began fast unto death outside the chief minister's residence.

Unaware of the developments between the chief minister and the opposition leaders, I received an urgent wireless message from deputy inspector general (DIG) of police (Intelligence) M.K. Shukla instructing me to proceed immediately to Bhopal for VIP security training, which I was obligated to attend. Without delay, I departed for Bhopal after instructing my subordinates to ensure peace and provide security to the agitators. Upon reaching Ujjain, I learnt that the chief minister had established a high-powered committee to investigate the incidents. The committee, comprising the principal secretary (Finance) and the inspector general of police (IG) [Research and Development], were scheduled to arrive in Neemuch for the investigation. I called the DIG to request the cancellation of the VIP security training as my presence before the committee was imperative. However, he insisted that I proceed to Bhopal. Thus, I complied, reassuring myself that everything was unfolding according to the will of God.

❧

Upon reaching Bhopal, I went directly to the DIG's office. After some time, I was summoned to his chamber. When I entered, the DIG remarked that he had intentionally kept me waiting to test my patience.

'My instincts tell me that you are a good officer with a clean record,' he said. 'I have spoken to your seniors and all of them have spoken highly of you. The massive agitation against you is merely a consequence of the challenging times.' He then introduced me to the then Director General of Police (DGP) M. Natarajan, who advised me not to be distressed as such incidents are a part of a policeman's career. He urged me to remain vigilant about future occurrences. I listened to his counsel attentively, yet I could not help but question, 'What is my fault in this entire episode?'

The DGP advised me to meet the chief minister the next day at 11 a.m. and arranged an appointment with him. As soon as I met the chief minister, he said, 'You do not seem to be what the rumours are circulating. Tell me what exactly happened.' I relayed the entire story.

After meeting the chief minister, I inquired about the training at the intelligence institute but came to know that there would be none. The objective of conveying such a message was only to summon me to Bhopal. I hastily left for Neemuch the very next day, knowing that I must present my case before the inquiry committee.

It was purely coincidental that just as I was about to set out for Neemuch via Ujjain, the inquiry committee came to Ujjain after conducting an initial investigation into the incident at Singoli. The committee members were scheduled to meet the commissioner and DIG at the Ujjain control room. Upon learning of this, I promptly made my way to the control room and met with the members of the probe committee.

The committee members stated that their investigation had concluded and that they had found no fault on my part: 'If the incident had taken place a few days later, allowing them to get familiar with your working style, they would not have singled you out. However, due to the rapid spread of the misinformation campaign, the local residents began demanding retribution from you unjustly. Nevertheless, we understand that you were not aware of the measures taken against the agitators.' The members of the committee then left for Bhopal.

It seemed that God was with me and I would be given a clean chit in connection with the first agitation against me in my police service career. I returned to Neemuch, where I was told that the Neemuch subdivision had been divided into two parts: Neemuch and Jawad. Jawad, which includes Singoli, was made a separate subdivision. I was made the city SP of Neemuch. An experienced officer was sent to Jawad as SDO of police. Thus, the government quelled the fire of agitation for a while.

❧

The opposition came to power after the assembly election, and the opposition party's president became the chief minister. I was appointed as deputy commandant of the 23rd Battalion in Bhopal. As per the prevailing cadre management system, newly recruited Indian Police Service (IPS) officers underwent training and were subsequently posted as SDOs of police in districts. Following this, they were assigned to larger districts as additional superintendents of police (ASPs).

Facing a transfer to what might be perceived as a non-significant position can be a challenging experience, especially when it is intended as a punishment. The sudden shift in responsibilities and reduced stature that came with the new role presented a unique set of challenges. However, I recognized that dwelling on the negative aspects of the situation would only impede my progress. Instead, I resolved to view this experience as an opportunity for personal growth and professional development. It is worth noting that setbacks and challenges are an inherent part of any professional journey. I continued as deputy commandant of the 23rd Battalion in Bhopal for two and a half years before being promoted to commandant.

Despite several of my batchmates and juniors being appointed as SPs in various districts, I was deprived of such an opportunity because of my punitive assignment. At the police headquarters I was told that the chief minister was displeased with me (as he had been told by his supporters that I was responsible for police atrocities in Singoli) and that he did not want me in any district.

I was posted as deputy commandant in the 23rd Battalion since the commandant did not originate from the IPS cadre. He had started his career in the SI cadre and later ascended to the rank of commandant while awaiting the IPS award. It was apparent that I was deliberately placed under the authority of my junior officer, who was subsequently granted the IPS cadre a year junior to my batch. The 23rd and 25th Battalions were on the same campus, and a senior lady IPS officer was the commandant of the 25th Battalion. However, I was not posted under her. The government's intention was clear.

I continued working without paying attention to such petty issues. There was a dog squad in the 23rd Battalion, so I started taking an interest in training dogs. Through the training I provided, the team became national champions. Additionally, there was a company of women constables, and people tended to look down upon them. I encouraged them to plant saplings and assigned specific areas for them to care for. As a result, the campus soon turned into a fine forest.

During that time, the then DGP never proposed my posting to a district. Whenever I attended meetings held by the home minister or chief minister, the seats next to me remained empty. Senior officers avoided sitting next to me out of fear of repercussions from the government. I was treated as persona non grata, seen as unsuitable for field postings. Many officers didn't even talk to me, contributing to my isolation within the department. Despite this, I found solace in activities like playing badminton and horse riding during my free time in the mornings and evenings.

Coincidentally, K.S. Rathore, a senior IPS officer, was posted to the training department in Bhopal. My horse-riding skills highly impressed him. He was an international-level horse rider and had won several national and international medals and awards; he also had a personal squad of horses. His love for horses was so deep that he even took his horse with him on deputation when posted with the Border Security Force, a first in the force's history.

Rathore started joining me for horse riding, and soon it became a regular activity for both of us, eventually leading me to give up playing badminton altogether. As we rode together, he got to know me better. An international horse-riding contest was organized and I commanded the opening ceremony, winning a medal. Rathore was so happy with me that he offered his personal mare Shefali to me as a gift. However, I politely declined as I had no place to keep a horse.

Fortunately, there was a change and Rathore assumed the position of DGP. The next day when I reached the riding arena, he told me to meet him in his office at 1 p.m. He said that he had some plans for me. Before meeting Rathore, I consulted with IG U.M. Joshi of the State Armed Forces, who informed me about the DGP's interest in meeting me.

Mr Joshi said, 'Rathore wants to set up a mounted battalion and make you its commandant, but you should not consent to it. Tell him that no other IPS officer would like to become the commandant of a mounted battalion after you. If he wants to do something good for you, he should send you to some district as SP. I have informed him that many of your juniors have already been appointed to such positions.'

When I went to meet Rathore, he expressed his desire to do something good for me. I conveyed my humiliation, citing that many of my juniors had surpassed me and become SPs. Rathore swiftly grasped my sentiments and even though he had had an alternative plan in mind, he agreed to consider my proposal. Immediately thereafter, he called up Additional Director General (ADG) [Intelligence] Narendra Prasad and instructed him to arrange a meeting between the chief minister and myself to dispel any doubts regarding my capabilities. Rathore emphasized that decades-long careers should not be allowed to go to waste and promised to personally discuss the matter with the chief minister.

As soon as my meeting with Rathore was over, I went to see Narendra Prasad who had already fixed my appointment with the chief minister. I was told to meet the officer on special duty at the chief minister's residence at 11 a.m. the next day. The officer would take me to the chief minister.

The next day, when I reached the place of my appointment, the officer on special duty had already sent my name to the chief minister, who promptly summoned me to his chamber. As soon as I appeared before the chief minister, he expressed his surprise saying, 'I thought Shailendra Srivastava would be a red-eyed officer with a big moustache, who created fear among people and fostered hatred against them. However, you appear to be very simple. So far, no one has spoken a good word about you, but today, now that you are in front of me, I think I recognize your true character.'

Immediately afterwards, the chief minister issued directives and I was appointed as SP and posted to Rajnandgaon, a Maoists' bastion. It was my first independent field posting. Some colleagues said, 'Either the Maoists will be wiped out or you will be. In either case, the government will be happy.' I prepared to confront the challenges head-on, viewing this opportunity as a chance to showcase my abilities. Over time, I succeeded in doing that.

Reflecting on this transition, I realized that encountering challenging phases is an inevitable part of life, but it is crucial to embrace them with grace.

4

Into the Heartland of Guerrilla Warfare

Maoists are known for their brutality and proficiency in handling explosives and modern weapons. Their expertise in guerrilla warfare and familiarity with forest paths make them formidable adversaries. Police officers posted in Maoist-infested areas face constant danger, with death lurking at every corner. However, their unwavering commitment to their profession drives them to respond to the call of duty, regardless of the risks involved.

In the remote corners of West Bengal lies a modest hamlet called Naxalbari that witnessed the birth of a revolutionary fire in 1967. Charu Majumdar and Kanu Sanyal, fervent Communist leaders, drew inspiration from the visionary ideals of China's communist leader Mao Zedong, igniting an armed revolution that resonated across the nation and came to define an entire era.

Unyielding in their pursuit of social justice, the Naxals cut ties with the Communist Party of India and formed the All India Coordination Committee of Communist Revolutionaries. They disappeared into the shadows, their actions shrouded in mystery and defiance. In the wake of Charu Majumdar's untimely demise, internal rebellions threatened to fracture the movement, leaving the Naxals at crossroads, their ideology being tested and their path uncertain.

Over time, new leaders emerged, each carrying the flame of revolution in their hearts. However, ideological differences led to factionalism, with varied interpretations of the movement's purpose spanning across states like Madhya Pradesh, Telangana, Chhattisgarh, Odisha, Jharkhand and Bihar. While some embraced the political avenues and participated in the very system they had fought against, others remained resolute in their underground struggles and clandestine activities.

Naxalism—once rooted in an ideology of revolutionary change and social justice—has, over the years, progressively transformed into a menacing force of lawless extortion, challenging the very essence of democratic governance. What initially stemmed from a vision of an equitable society has now become a serious threat, disrupting normalcy and endangering communities.

Police officers deployed in Maoist-infested regions endure harsh working conditions and have to navigate challenging terrains, such as hilly areas, narrow dusty lanes in remote villages and dense forests. They carry rifles and heavy backpacks, tirelessly marching for miles without rest or proper meals. Comfort is a luxury they seldom experience. These adverse conditions are essential precautions against the hidden dangers posed by the Claymore mines and landmines planted by the Maoists.

I experienced these challenges when I was stationed in Rajnandgaon, formerly a district in Madhya Pradesh and now in Chhattisgarh. Rajnandgaon is surrounded by the Durg, Balaghat, Mandla and Bastar districts of Madhya Pradesh; Gadchiroli, Chandrapur and Bhandara districts of Maharashtra; and Khammam district of Telangana. The area is highly sensitive due to the presence of Maoists.

Except for Durg, all forested districts were considered red zones where police officers and locals had lost their lives in IED (improvised explosive device) blasts orchestrated by the Naxals. Being posted in this dangerous zone was a personal challenge. I boarded the Chhattisgarh Express from Bhopal to reach this perilous region. Coincidentally, an assistant sub-inspector (ASI) boarded the train at the Gondia railway station in Maharashtra and sat beside me. He had no idea who I was or where I was headed. Out of curiosity, I asked him quietly if we had entered the red zone yet. In a hushed tone, he cautioned, 'Do not speak of it, or they will overhear you.'

The ASI's words revealed the deep fear that police officers and citizens had of the Maoists. At that time, I had limited knowledge about Maoists, but his remark made me suspect that there was more to the situation than met the eye.

Upon arriving in Rajnandgaon and assuming the role of SP, I discovered that the police force had no records or written documents regarding Maoist groups. We lacked information about their network, communication systems, activities, leaders and the size of their membership, their support systems and the weaponry they possessed. Furthermore, the police force was unfamiliar with conducting operations against the Maoists, navigating the forests, gaining the trust of the locals and, most importantly, dealing with booby traps.

To address these critical gaps, I organized meetings with experienced police officers and officials from other departments. N.K. Singh (IG, Bhilai) possessed extensive experience in conducting operations against organized gangs, and he imparted his knowledge to me on how to effectively combat the Naxal menace. As a result, I was able to compile a comprehensive record of the Maoists and their activities. Using this valuable intelligence, I initiated numerous operations against the Maoists and directly engaged with them. Through these encounters, we were able to devise effective strategies and tools to counter this threat. I also sought the cooperation of village heads and community members, who initially hesitated due to fear of the Maoists. I assured them that the police were there to protect them and emphasized the importance of not succumbing to fear. Gradually, some individuals came forward to help. Through their assistance, we began uncovering the Maoists' recruitment methods and operational tactics.

Rajnandgaon district, a place of pristine natural beauty, offers abundant natural resources, art, music, literature and archaeological findings. However, the arrival of Maoists disrupted the lives of the local populace, leading to unrest and instability.

The local tribal population relies on agriculture and forest produce for their livelihood. However, they face restrictions from forest officials for extracting resources from the forests. Exploiting the situation, Maoists have positioned themselves as supporters of the tribal people, offering help and challenging the authority of the forest department. This has allowed them to gain considerable influence in the area. Nevertheless, the police and district administration are making efforts to combat the Maoist presence, indicating a potential future where they will be eradicated from the region.

During police operations against the Maoists, the strategy is adjusted to navigate the challenging terrain and avoid traps set by the Maoists. The police employ high tension lines and topographic sheets and carry provisions like roasted gram and water to sustain themselves. They camp in tents in the forests instead of resting in government buildings or rest houses. The police have developed techniques to handle snakes, scorpions and wild animals, and they have also established ways to ambush the Maoists, navigate landmines, gain the trust of locals and ensure the effectiveness of their information network.

While preparing for the civil services, I studied the history of India, particularly the guerrilla warfare tactics employed by historical figures such as Chhatrapati Shivaji Maharaj, Malik Ambar and Maharana Pratap. I also learnt about the guerrilla tactics used by Mao Zedong during the Chinese Communist Revolution in 1949 and Che Guevara's role in the Cuban revolution and his fight against the US Army in Vietnam. I incorporated these learnings while training my forces and emphasized the importance of adapting to local conditions before implementing such tactics.

One method employed by Maoists was the formation of a committee called Sangam. This committee consists of villagers who hold meetings with the youth and promote Maoist ideology by discussing the heroic deeds of their ideologues. Sangam members also provide food to the Maoists during their visits to the villages and inform them about the movement of security forces. As the Sangam members gain expertise in guerrilla warfare by collaborating with Maoists, they are enlisted into the Dalam, which is a subdivision within the Maoist organization. With the assistance of Sangam members, the Dalam members set booby traps targeting police officers and then seize weapons from incapacitated or deceased officers during skirmishes. Additionally, the Maoists acquire firearms from various sources, including engagements with terrorists and arms suppliers and by confiscating licensed weapons from local villagers.

Operating primarily in hilly and forested areas, Maoist units employ a staggered formation during movement, with one member leading and another following closely behind while maintaining some distance from each other. Their activities are known to diminish in the rainy season due to impassable forest paths, yet they intermittently exploit the common belief that they are in hibernation during this time by conducting surprise operations and launching attacks on security outposts in remote areas where immediate medical aid is difficult to provide.

Financially, the Maoists amass funds from various sources. They extort money from government employees and contractors involved in the tendu leaf trade. Additionally, they target mining companies within their sphere of influence for financial gains.

Near the Rajnandgaon border lies Darrekasa, a small village in the Salekasa administrative division of Gondia district, Maharashtra. Surrounded by dense forests and located near the Mumbai–Kolkata railway tracks, the village is home to a railway station where a group of 12 extremists once launched an attack on a Special Reserve Police post.

The police post, which had 15 officers stationed there, was carefully observed by the Maoists prior to the attack. They discovered that five police officers from the outpost patrolled nearby villages between 7 and 8 p.m. Two officers prepared food, one stayed on guard duty while the rest were engaged in casual conversations. The forested area was approximately 500 m away from the outpost.

The extremists devised a plan to thoroughly explore the forested surroundings before sunset and then advance and take up strategic positions once night fell. They scheduled the operation to commence at 7.30 p.m. and conclude within half an hour. Additionally, they aimed to seize the weapons stored at the outpost. The extremists fired a total of 366 bullets but the determined police officers, despite being outnumbered and outgunned, managed to defend their position. Their resilience, which resulted in the death of one extremist and injuries to another, forced the Maoists to retreat. Three police officers were also injured during the attack.

The Maoists realized their mistake and designated two members to analyse their errors to prevent similar blunders in future operations. According to their assessment, the commander of the raiding party should have thoroughly examined the plan before execution and based the attack on the information gathered during the survey. The decision to hastily approach the post proved fatal because several raiding party members stumbled into the fencing surrounding the police outpost, thereby removing the element of surprise they had intended to achieve. Had they refrained from proceeding with the attack after their initial plan failed, their situation might have been more favourable. Being alerted the moment the raiders collided with the fence, the police officers got ample time to prepare for the assault.

The presence of 15 officers at the outpost combined with wireless communication to arrange additional reinforcements enabled the police officers to remain composed and force the Maoists to retreat after a fierce gun battle. Once the raiders realized that they could not overpower the police and that their surprise attack had failed, the commander should have advised them to maintain their positions outside, engage in gunfire, throw hand grenades and then retreat. Initially, when the commander ordered his men to advance, they opened fire. However, according to the original plan, the commander was supposed to assess the situation before giving the order to fire. Conventional wisdom in guerrilla warfare suggests that raiders should strike their enemies swiftly to achieve victory. In this attack, the extremists fired upon the police officers who were positioned 35 m away from them, but had they moved more cautiously, they would have noticed the fencing and avoided stumbling into it.

Another significant error made by the Naxals was their deputy commander's decision to instruct his men to enter the premises of the police outpost and crawl, which caused a delay. Instead, one or two raiders had to provide cover fire, while the rest should have swiftly reached the camp wall. If they had done so, they would have had an opportunity to throw hand grenades through the windows from which the police officers were firing. This could have given the Maoists an advantage. Experts suggest that fighters should not crawl in open fields or when they are near the enemy. When a team launches an attack, they should assess the situation on the ground and adapt accordingly instead of rigidly adhering to a specific method.

Due to their failure to survey the area, the Maoist attackers remained confined to one location. Consequently, they were unable to attack the police officers from different sides, resulting in diminished assault intensity. Many extremists experienced weapon malfunctions during the attack, which had also occurred in previous incidents. Thus, they realized the importance of properly maintaining their firearms.

Furthermore, contrary to the commander's advice, the Maoists expended more ammunition than necessary, which ultimately worked against them.

After thoroughly investigating and analysing this incident, we implemented revisions and redesigns to our security protocols for the police outposts.

❧

The extent of brutality exhibited by Maoists is unfathomable to the average person. In situations where they suspect someone of being a police informant, their actions are shockingly ruthless. One such incident occurred in Bagrekasa village in Rajnandgaon. The Maoists were suspicious about a man who had allegedly collaborated with the police, and a fellow villager may have provided this information to the extremists. During the night, they launched a raid on the village with the intention of executing the accused. They forcibly pulled him out of his house, decapitated him and gruesomely displayed his body by hanging it upside down from a bamboo structure. To further instil terror, they axed off the man's right hand and, using his arm as a macabre tool, wrote a chilling message on the wall of his own house with his own blood, warning all informers that they would suffer the same fate. The Maoists deliberately left behind the victim's severed head and hand as a grim reminder for the villagers. This horrific incident served as a clear demonstration of the Maoists' barbarity. They intended to deter any assistance to or cooperation with the police by instilling fear in the hearts of the villagers.

While conducting routine foot patrolling in the Naxalite-infested areas in 1993, we reached Dangbora village, notorious for Maoist activities. Amidst its wilderness was a rest house belonging to the irrigation department where we decided to rest for the night.

As the clock struck ten, Tota and Myna approached us in the darkness. Former Naxals, they had forsaken their past to become constables in the police force. They urged us not to stay in the rest house, saying, 'The Naxals, cunning as serpents, plant lethal bombs in such rest houses. We must seek shelter elsewhere, perhaps in the sanctuary of the school.'

Since their past affiliations provided them with intimate knowledge about the workings of the extremist groups, we decided to heed their counsel and sought refuge in a nearby school building. The Naxals, who were aware of our presence in the village and had been waiting to unleash their attack, were taken by surprise when they found the rest house empty. Oblivious that we had taken shelter in the school building, they bombed the rest house, reducing it to rubble. We had miraculously survived only because of Tota and Myna's timely warning.

Tragically, the story took a grim turn as Tota and Myna became targets of relentless pursuit by vengeful Naxals.

Despite seeking refuge in their home district of Bastar, Tota and Myna were unable to escape from the clutches of the Naxals. The Naxals caught up with them and exacted their revenge.

In the wake of this heinous act, we were profoundly saddened and vowed to seek justice in their memory.

❧

The extremists regularly visited a weekly market to purchase essential supplies, such as milk powder, tea leaves, groceries, newspapers and medicines. Upon discovering their routine, we hatched a plan to apprehend them right there in the market.

My fellow officers and I disguised ourselves as villagers to covertly surround the Naxals. We set up small shops where we sold tea leaves, milk powder and other items. Underneath a piece of cloth spread on the ground, we concealed AK-47 rifles, positioning ourselves strategically on the same cloth.

During one of these market visits, the deputy commander of the Naxals, Shyam Rao, also known as Bhumaiya Sarvaille Gopanna, appeared. Upon receiving a signal from an informant, I seized the opportunity and apprehended the commander. I moved swiftly, grabbed him and placed an AK-47 rifle against his chest. With my colleagues also quickly joining in, we subdued him and ensured his capture.

Shyam Rao was the deputy commander of the Tanda group, also known as Tanda Dalam. Following his arrest, demands arose from an adjoining state, urging us to hand him over. Allegedly, he had been involved in a devastating explosion that had claimed the lives of 24 individuals. Authorities from the neighbouring state even offered us two Naxals armed with AK-47 rifles in exchange for the deputy commander, suggesting that we could claim credit for a successful anti-Naxal operation by showcasing their arrest within our jurisdiction. However, I firmly refused this proposition.

Recognizing the gravity of the situation, I promptly informed the then ADG of Intelligence, A.N. Pathak, about the offer and the pressure being exerted on us from the neighbouring state. Given our collaborative efforts with police forces from neighbouring states, it was crucial to proceed with caution. Pathak took the matter up with the chief minister, who, during a session in the state assembly, publicly announced the successful arrest of a hardcore Naxal leader by the police. This not only helped us maintain a positive relationship with the police forces of other states but also ensured that we stayed on the right side of the law.

On a fateful evening in 1993, as the sun descended upon the dangerous hillocks of Kalghurra, Praveer Tiwari, commander of Lalbagh police station, and I embarked on a perilous mission against the Maoists. The terrain demanded a gruelling 25-km trek, but the mesmerizing waterfalls and untamed beauty softened the burden of our journey. The enchanting foliage and enigmatic darkness of the dense forest had drawn the attention of the Naxals, who found solace in these hills. As we ventured further, we stumbled upon the remnants of their presence: discarded remains of hunted peacocks and scattered traces of food. Amongst these fragments, we discovered curious artefacts, such as soaps, pliers and even the vibrant bindis worn by Naxalite women.

Night fell and we set up camp, deciding to resume our search the following day. Praveer discovered that his AK-47 rifle was malfunctioning; its mechanical intricacies had succumbed to the strain of our mission. Suddenly, Praveer advanced towards the firearm because his curiosity was piqued. In that instant, I instinctively sprang into action. Moving with the swiftness of a cheetah, I forcefully yanked him away from the imminent danger.

Our bodies collided, and we crashed to the ground. Time seemed to stand still.

In the blink of an eye, it happened—the deafening crack of the rifle echoed through the air, shattering the silence. By some miraculous twist of fate, the bullets spared him, veering away from their deadly trajectory. Praveer had narrowly escaped the clutches of death, and the harrowing encounter left us both shaken to our very core.

In that surreal moment, we realized the fragility of life and the delicate balance between survival and death. As we gathered our wits, we vowed to continue our mission with determination, forever grateful for the narrow escape that fate had bestowed upon us. This incident underscored the importance of vigilance and quick thinking in the face of danger and the need for resilience in challenging situations.

❧

In the small village of Bortalab, SI Suraj Jagirdar was known for his expertise in treating snakebite cases and held a position of authority within the force.

However, whispers of discontent against the officer began echoing throughout the village as the villagers grew weary of their encounters with the SI, who allegedly used his position to harass and exploit women under the guise of snakebite treatments. Their grievances mounted until they could no longer be ignored. Finally, an inquiry was launched, which revealed the shocking truth. Swift and decisive action was taken, and Suraj Jagirdar was suspended from duty.

When I reviewed the case, I recognized the gravity of the situation. In the SI's annual confidential report, I documented the deep-seated resentment harboured against him by the people in the areas where he had been posted. It was clear that caution had to be exercised to prevent any further turmoil. Aware of the dangerous landscape we navigated, I warned against posting the disgraced police officer to any Naxal-infested area. I feared that the locals' seething anger, if harnessed by the extremists, could lead to a catastrophic attack on our forces.

During my inspection of the Manpur police station, I predicted that if any police station in Rajnandgaon district were to be attacked, it would undoubtedly be Manpur. My intimate knowledge of the Maoists' tactics had allowed me to paint a grim picture of how they could execute their assault.

I envisioned the extremists descending upon the weekly market, meticulously surveying the area before taking cover in the hillocks that faced the police station. The following morning, while it was still dark, they would strike with ruthless precision. Relying on my intuition, I implemented robust defences by employing ingenious measures, which included keeping stray dogs, spreading dry leaves around the police stations and erecting trident-like barriers made of bamboo sticks. These deterrents would make it difficult for the Naxals to silently approach our stations. Additionally, I oversaw the construction of scaffoldings atop the tallest trees to provide vantage points for our officers to fire upon the assailants. Strong barbed wire fences were erected to fortify the perimeter, and hidden tunnels were meticulously crafted to ensure quick and stealthy escape. The maps were marked with the Naxals' potential paths of infiltration.

However, before I could witness the first-hand impact of my efforts, I was transferred to Sagar, leaving the arduous task of safeguarding Manpur in the hands of a new officer.

The new officer revoked SI Suraj Jagirdar's suspension and posted the disgraced officer as the station house officer of Manpur. Regrettably, SI Suraj Jagirdar failed to heed the lessons from his previous suspension and persisted in his troubling behaviour of harassing villagers and exploiting their women. Disappointed and disillusioned, the villagers, who had initially looked to the police for justice, found themselves consumed by dissatisfaction. They sought solace in an unexpected alliance and turned to the Naxals to avenge their grievances.

Days turned into nights as the Naxals meticulously executed their plans just as I had assumed. They frequented the market—their presence went unnoticed during the day—and sought refuge in the hillocks by night. With the first light of dawn, their assault unfolded, catching the ill-prepared police force off guard because the arrangements I had kept in place were all removed.

Suraj Jagirdar had been sleeping soundly in the safety of his home, oblivious to the impending danger. The Maoists assaulted him and stormed the police station. Their nefarious intentions became clear as they looted a cache of formidable weapons, including AK-47 rifles, self-loading rifles, light machine guns and an abundance of ammunition. Finally, to erase any evidence of their brazen act, they mercilessly obliterated the police station, leaving behind only destruction and despair.

The once-proud Manpur police station lay in ruins, a testament to the tragic consequences of neglecting the warnings that I had meticulously noted in my report.

❧

As the SP of Rajnandgaon, I gained a thorough understanding of the dangers that lurked in every shadow. It was my duty to ensure the safety of my comrades and guide them away from the jaws of peril.

Through my personal experience and extensive visits to various spots of Naxalite incidents, coupled with a deep understanding of

Maoist strategies and shortcomings revealed through the literature seized from them, we embarked on a mission to design foolproof strategies to survive and control the looming threat of Naxalism. Our determination led us to unveil innovative tactics that would not only safeguard our communities but also outsmart the Maoists at their own game.

We implemented several strategies to counter the Maoists. One such strategy involved integrating trained dogs as early warning systems to bolster our defence. These dogs possessed acute sense to detect intruders and were stationed at police outposts and stations.

Another tactic employed was the scattering of dry leaves throughout the precincts to create an auditory minefield. The distinctive crunch of footsteps on the leaves shattered the silence, alerting us to potential intruders. Additionally, we erected bamboo tridents along the boundaries, positioning their tips outward to create a formidable barrier; this made crawling a risky endeavour during relentless Maoist onslaughts.

Furthermore, we fortified the perimeter by setting up strong barbed wire fences. Scaffoldings were built atop the tallest trees within the police station premises to offer vantage points for our officers to open fire on assailants. Moreover, intricate underground tunnels were constructed within police stations. These tunnels served as hidden vantage points, enabling officers to strategically position themselves and confront the Naxals head-on. Connected to the storerooms and armouries, they ensured a steady supply of weapons and ammunition during the relentless onslaught by Maoists.

Drawing from my experiences, here are some potential strategies that can assist the administration in effectively addressing the Naxal issue.

Firstly, establishing a committee comprising representatives from different units in Naxal-infested areas and affected states can facilitate coordination and collaboration in decision-making processes. This committee would tackle administrative hurdles and implement development initiatives aimed at fostering a sense of ownership and empowerment among communities, thereby reducing susceptibility to Maoist influence.

Secondly, assigning honest and efficient officers to Maoist-affected areas would strengthen the administration in those regions. Addressing conflicts among tribal communities fairly and expeditiously and equipping judges with adequate resources to handle disputes efficiently would disrupt Naxal influence channels that work under the guise of dispute resolution.

Additionally, prioritizing education and healthcare services in tribal areas improves living standards and provides opportunities for economic growth, thus reducing vulnerability to Maoist recruitment tactics. Furthermore, ensuring that tribal people benefit from welfare schemes protecting their rights, particularly regarding land and forest resources, is crucial. Creating jobs for locals through forest produce-based cottage industries and small-scale enterprises can reduce economic disparities and minimize exploitation.

Efforts to curb alcohol availability can also reduce social problems associated with substance abuse, strengthening community resilience against extremist influences.

Finally, targeting the financial resources of Naxal groups can weaken their operational capabilities and reduce their influence in tribal areas. Strong political will and government involvement at all levels are crucial for the successful implementation of anti-Naxal measures.

Above all, it is important to recognize that the fight against Naxalism is ongoing. Thus, maintaining vigilance and adaptability is essential for effectively countering evolving Maoist tactics.

Through coordinated and organized implementation of these measures, the government can make significant progress in resolving the Naxal issue and bringing peace and development to affected regions.

In recent times, governments have recognized the severity of the issue and are prioritizing efforts to combat Naxalism. Realizing that the threat posed by Naxalism transcends mere security concerns, administrative bodies have undertaken multifaceted strategies to tackle the underlying socioeconomic disparities fuelling the movement, aiming for a comprehensive solution to this complex challenge.

5

The Parcel Bomb

Every police officer carries the weighty responsibility of apprehending criminals and ensuring the protection of the innocent. However, given that criminals often possess an understanding of the legal system, they frequently manage to evade conviction. Consequently, safeguarding the freedom of an innocent individual from unwarranted imprisonment remains a truly fulfilling endeavour.

While posted in Bilaspur as SP, I had gone to Bhopal to attend a conference of collectors and SPs, which was addressed by the chief minister. On my way back, upon reaching the Bilaspur station at 5.30 a.m., I was surprised to find a large contingent of officers and staff, including the ASP, city SP, police station in-charge and several cops, waiting to receive me.

I asked the ASP the reason for the presence of such a large number of cops at the station. He informed me that a parcel bomb had exploded at a public call office (PCO) in the city the previous evening, resulting in the tragic death of a young woman. He further said that the police had already detained Sardarji, the owner of the PCO, at the Civil Lines police station. My staff and I immediately went to the blast site. As a police officer, I believe that any case, however complicated it may be, can be cracked if it is investigated properly. We arrived at the location in 10 minutes.

⤝⤞

The explosion had occurred in a PCO that also sold electronic goods. Someone had sent the owner, Sardarji, a parcel. The post office had called him, asking him to collect the parcel, but as he did not go there to receive it, the postman had come to deliver it to his shop.

A young woman working at the PCO accepted the delivery on Sardarji's behalf and informed him about it over the phone. Sardarji instructed the woman to open the parcel to see what was in it. The woman had just opened the packet when it exploded with a deafening bang, killing her.

The chain of events forced the inquiry officer to conclude that Sardarji himself had sent the parcel to the PCO and asked the woman to open it, so when she did, it blew up. Someone had planned to murder the woman and the evidence pointed the needle of doubt towards Sardarji.

While the possibility of Maoists being behind the blast couldn't be entirely ruled out, considering their increasing activity in the area, it was puzzling why they would target a PCO owned by Sardarji. They could have easily registered their presence by triggering a blast in a public place. Nonetheless, Sardarji was taken into custody as the cops were sure that he had committed the crime, but I was opposed to this viewpoint.

☙

The scene at the PCO was harrowing. It was dreadful to witness the deceased's body parts stuck to the walls and the floor speckled with blood. The blast had destroyed all the items in the PCO, resulting in significant financial loss. The scene almost numbed me.

I called for Sardarji and a forensic team to the spot. While inspecting the shop, I noticed bloodstained currency notes and coins lying scattered. Sardarji's behaviour shocked me—despite the presence of maggots, he began to gather the bloodstained, currency notes and coins. I thought that someone indifferent to collecting even bloodstained currency notes is unlikely to orchestrate a crime that would result in significant financial loss to him.

I called the in-charge of the crime branch to the spot and set up a special team to investigate the case. At the outset, we examined the parcel that had exploded. Though it was in smithereens, we were able to piece together most of the parts.

Upon closer inspection, we discovered that a gelatine stick had been placed inside a nine-inch microphone, containing small iron nails, ball bearings and detonators. The detonator was connected to a AA battery and a pressure switch from a refrigerator was used to ignite the battery. This IED had been concealed within the microphone pack.

We also studied the paper that had been used to cover the parcel; it had 'CWN' written on it. Initially, we thought that the parcel may have come from the Maoist-infested area of Kanker, but the post office staff said that 'CWN' signified Kanpur, which too was suffering from terrorism. One of my colleagues suggested that terrorists could have sent the parcel with the intention of killing Sardarji. I was sure that Sardarji was innocent, but because he had already been taken into custody, people would have questioned my integrity had I ordered his release.

We decided to visit the victim's house. Her family members had taken her body to the cremation ground after the post-mortem and had just returned home. While searching her room, I came across a letter that was perhaps written by a jilted lover. The letter said, 'I may have stopped keeping any arms but I can still use them. I've tried to meet you several times but he prevented me.' It was unclear from the letter who the referred-to 'he' was; the family members also could not help determine the author of the letter.

After going through the letter, three possibilities struck me: terrorists might have tried to kill Sardarji due to some connection; a jilted lover might have killed the woman; or Sardarji's character might have been dubious, leading him to harm the woman upon seeing her with another boy.

I set up three separate teams to work on these three points. On reaching the control room, we held a discussion and decided to revisit the woman's residence in the evening to meet her family members.

We arrived at her house at 8 p.m. and spoke with her father and mother separately. They informed us that the girl had befriended a boy named Pramod, whose father was an inspector at the wireless department of the police. The parents couldn't confirm whether their daughter had only been acquainted with the boy or been romantically involved with him.

When we questioned Sardarji about the boy, he denied having any knowledge about the victim's affair. It was concerning that microphones similar to the one used to make the bomb were available in his shop. It now seemed that Sardarji had indeed sent the bomb.

❦

The next morning, I sent another team to the victim's house to collect further information about the boy. Her sister confirmed the details we had received earlier and added that the boy lived either in Durg or Bastar. I dispatched Assistant SP Chanchal Shekhar to Durg to locate Pramod. From the office of the SP (Wireless), he came to know that Pramod was the son of Inspector Ramesh Chandra.

When Pramod's father abandoned his mother and married another woman, Pramod had filed written complaints with various government departments about the matter. We learnt that Pramod had departed for Bhopal to personally lodge complaints with senior police officers and ministers. He was scheduled to meet the SP (Radio), Bhilai, after having already filed a complaint with them regarding his father's remarriage. Given these circumstances, we had no option but to await his return.

After talking to the deceased's sister, I was sure that Pramod had sent the parcel bomb to kill Sardarji but, unfortunately, it killed the woman instead. Despite my conviction, I did not share my thoughts with anyone except Chanchal Shekhar, whom I had assigned the task of apprehending Pramod.

Later that night, I took Sardarji into confidence and told him that I knew he was not the culprit, explaining that his temporary custody was only to manage media attention. We allowed him to go home to eat and take a bath. My behaviour impressed Sardarji so much that his eyes moistened and he was ready to cooperate with the police. Sardarji disclosed that a boy named Pramod used to harass the victim, for which he had scolded the youth several times. When I asked him why he had concealed this information, Sardarji admitted that fear of the police had compelled him to feign ignorance.

I instructed Assistant SP Chanchal Shekhar to stay in Bhilai and wait for Pramod. However, the prolonged search and lack of progress incited resentment among the locals, who grew impatient with the delay in solving the bomb blast, which was the first of its kind in the area. Moreover, a few officers of the district began questioning my efficiency and working style. They believed that there was no reason to continue the search when a suspect had already been taken into custody.

The team that had been sent to Kanpur interviewed the window clerk of the post office from where the parcel had been sent. The clerk said an individual had come to the counter with a parcel with the receiver's address typed on it but not the sender's. When he advised the sender to write his address, he wrote only 'Ram Bagh, Kanpur'; the CWN postal code was then written by the duty clerk. I told the team to stay in Kanpur and wait for further instructions.

When Pramod reached the office of the SP (Radio) in Bhilai after five days, Chanchal Shekhar informed me and I told him to bring Pramod to Bilaspur for questioning. Pramod came along without any resistance. The next day, he was interrogated by the TI, who used traditional methods to make Pramod speak, but he remained silent.

I was sure that Pramod had murdered the woman, so I called upon a reserve inspector (RI), who was honest and sincere, and known for his unconventional approach—he had a peculiar habit of giving weird replies without regard to the questions asked. Even though I had advised him to give up this habit, he stuck to it. I decided to use him to irritate Pramod, instructing him to vex Pramod throughout the night and deprive him of sleep. He did exactly as I said.

The RI nattered with him throughout the night, so much that Pramod got fed up with the irrelevant question–answer session and finally confessed to sending the parcel bomb. The murderer was so ruffled that he even told the RI to call the SP, promising to disclose everything. The RI called me at 4.15 a.m. and I went to see him at 4.30 a.m. As we conversed, Pramod divulged the true story behind his actions.

❧

Pramod said he had fallen in love with the woman but Sardarji used to come in the way and never let him meet her. The woman also refused to meet Pramod because he was unemployed; further, he was fed up with his family problems, which had taken a toll on his mental health.

One day, he found a book titled *Circuit* in a book stall at the Jabalpur railway station, which described the construction of a parcel bomb. His father was a wireless officer, so Pramod had access to microphones at home; he got the gelatine and detonators from mining department officials.

Pramod assembled the bomb and used a pressure switch from a refrigerator to trigger it. Once it was ready, he kept the bomb with him for a few days. In the meantime, he went to Seoni to complain about his father to the home minister. He then travelled from Seoni to Jabalpur and later to Lucknow to catch a bus to Kanpur, from where he dispatched the parcel bomb to Bilaspur.

Once the bomb exploded at the PCO, Pramod visited Bilaspur, discovering that Sardarji was alive but the woman had lost her life. When he was sure that Sardarji had been taken into police custody, he relaxed and continued his campaign against his father. He never thought that the police would collar him, but as soon as Assistant SP Chanchal Shekhar caught hold of him, Pramod realized that it was all over for him.

With the truth revealed, we released Sardarji and sent him back home because we had finally caught the real culprit behind the Bilaspur blast.

6

Web of Deception

A cunning criminal, scheming to extort money from a businessman, found himself behind bars as a dedicated team of police officers steadfastly pursued the case.

The heat was relentless as I settled into my new office as the DIG in the Crime Investigation Department (CID) in Bhopal. While I was occupied at my desk, a well-dressed gentleman sought permission from my personal secretary to discuss his grievances with me.

The man appeared visibly uneasy and troubled, reflecting his state of mind. Recognizing his discomfort, I swiftly requested the office boy to fetch a glass of water for him. Taking it upon myself, I prepared a cup of tea and offered it to the visitor. My composed demeanour and the attentive behaviour of my staff worked together to alleviate his anxiety. Finally, with a deep breath, the man mustered the courage to introduce himself as Shobhit Ashudani, a road construction contractor and owner of an engineering college.

Ashudani stated that he had signed a contract with the government to construct a road in the Badi area of Raisen district, Madhya Pradesh, and the project was already under way. However, he claimed that an individual named Mumtaz had falsely accused him of attempted murder. Mumtaz had also been extorting money from Ashudani's workers. Ashudani mentioned that he had recently tried to confront Mumtaz but was unsuccessful. Shockingly, Mumtaz filed an attempt to murder case against Ashudani, two days after their failed meeting, while being treated at Hamidia Hospital in Bhopal for severe acid burns.

According to Mumtaz's statement, he had been standing near the Badi–Bareli road when three individuals on a red motorcycle approached him, carrying a bucket of acid. They forced him into immersing his hands in the acid, resulting in severe injuries. One of them also allegedly warned him against harassing Ashudani and threatened to kill him. Mumtaz asserted that he recognized these three individuals as Ashudani's associates.

Ashudani claimed that the police had registered a case of

attempted murder against him and three others based on the evidence presented. Furthermore, he mentioned that the person who used to inspect the construction site on his behalf owned a red motorcycle.

All the evidence seemed to implicate Ashudani and his alleged accomplices. Had an investigation been conducted into Mumtaz's statement, the road contractor and three individuals would have been incarcerated. However, Ashudani vehemently denied these allegations, asserting that neither he nor his workers were involved in such a horrific act. His demeanour during our conversation suggested a man of integrity and averse to conflict. He appeared to be a businessman who earned his livelihood without engaging in conflict with others; he was even willing to offer a small sum of money to maintain peace and avoid disputes.

Once he left my office, I discussed the case with CID Inspector B.B. Sharma. He contacted the Badi police station and was informed that a case had been registered against Ashudani and three others for attempted murder. The Badi police station in-charge also informed Sharma that Mumtaz had several criminal cases filed against him at the Noor Bagh police station in Bhopal and operated in multiple areas, including Badi, Bareli, Salamatpur, Raisen, Gairatganj and Begumganj. Mumtaz was known for extorting money from businessmen. The Badi police station had registered a case against Ashudani because committing a crime against a wrongdoer is also wrong. Ashudani was served a notice in this regard.

Believing in Ashudani's innocence, I felt that the case should be transferred to the CID. I informed ADG Anand Kumar about this important issue through the intercom. He promptly called me to his chamber, where I presented Ashudani's application and provided information about his character and Mumtaz's criminal background. I also informed him that Mumtaz, who had allegedly suffered an acid attack, was admitted to Hamidia Hospital. I expressed to Kumar that the case was complex and that transferring it to the CID would help uncover the real culprits. Kumar agreed with me and authorized the transfer of the case.

Upon returning to my office, I instructed Sharma to locate the ward in Hamidia Hospital where Mumtaz was admitted.

'We will go there,' I told Sharma.

At the hospital, we observed that both of Mumtaz's hands were severely burnt. The doctors informed us that his hands needed to be amputated. I spoke to Mumtaz about the case, and he reiterated the same story that he had mentioned in his statement. Mumtaz also claimed that he did not have a mobile phone, making it quite challenging to track his movements.

Upon returning to the office, I reached out to a senior official at Bharat Sanchar Nigam Limited (BSNL), seeking the call detail records of Ashudani. Subsequently, we journeyed to Badi and eventually reached the local police station.

The TI of Badi confirmed the information he had shared with Sharma over the phone. Without wasting time, we visited the crime scene. I also summoned the witness, Maqshood, who lived in Bhopal. Maqshood's story corroborated Mumtaz's. Maqshood added that as soon as the trio fled, he approached the spot and took Mumtaz to a private hospital in Bhopal. However, the doctors there refused admission due to it being a criminal case and directed them to Hamidia Hospital.

When we inspected the construction site, we found the red motorcycle belonging to Ashudani's worker. Upon questioning Ashudani's workers about the incident, they denied having any knowledge of it. They stated that Ashudani had visited the site in his car three days earlier and had left after discussing about Mumtaz with them. Ashudani only became aware of the incident a day later.

❧

After examining the crime scene, we returned to the Badi police station and discussed the case with the staff. They suspected Ashudani's involvement in the attack based on Maqshood's testimony, Mumtaz's statement and the burns on his hands.

Back in Bhopal, I again summoned Maqshood to the CID office to officially document his statement. Despite his denial of owning a mobile phone, the intelligence gathered from CID informants revealed his linked mobile number. Maqshood's apparent lack of transparency regarding the possession of a mobile phone heightened my suspicions, casting doubt on the reliability of his statements. Consequently, we moved forward with the request for Maqshood's call detail records from BSNL.

The following day, at 11 a.m., I dispatched Sharma to the telephone office to gather the necessary information. Upon analysing the call details, I discovered that Ashudani had been at Arera Colony in Bhopal at the time of the incident. This contradicted Mumtaz's and Maqshood's statements, suggesting discrepancies in their testimonies.

Furthermore, at 10.30 p.m., approximately five to six hours after the incident, according to his call detail records, Maqshood had been in a village under the jurisdiction of the Gyaraspur police station.

This particular detail baffled me, and I wondered why Maqshood had not mentioned anything about being in Gyaraspur in his statement. On further questioning, Mumtaz also did not say anything about Maqshood's presence at Gyaraspur. He only reiterated that he did not keep a mobile phone with him and was unaware of why Maqshood's call details showed his location to be at Gyaraspur.

I again called Maqshood to the CID office to get some more information about the incident, but he stuck to his original statement, reiterating what he had already stated.

Failing to extract any new information from Mumtaz or Maqshood, we decided to go to Gyaraspur. When we reached our destination, night had already fallen.

My team members and I discussed Mumtaz's activities and background with the staff of the Gyaraspur police station. They informed us that Mumtaz, although not frequently seen in the area anymore, was known for extorting money from businessmen. I wanted to browse the general diary of the police station and ask the staff whether there had been any crime in the area recently. When I inquired whether Mumtaz had been seen in the area in the last few days, they denied it.

As I was sifting through the diary, a note on a page drew my attention. Just a day after the Badi incident, the kotwar (guard) of a nearby village had informed the police station that a band of robbers had struck a house at night when an explosion was heard. As the sound woke up the family of the house owner, the burglars had run away. We decided to go to the village where the blast had occurred. On reaching there, I called the village kotwar and we went with him to the house that the robbers had tried to rob. The villagers confirmed the attempted burglary and recounted how the burglars fled after the explosion.

Though my team members did not find anything suspicious, a few ball bearings and iron nails were strewn at the spot where the blast had occurred and the smell of gunpowder still hung in the air.

I suddenly realized that when I had examined Mumtaz's hands at the hospital, I had smelt gunpowder. However, I kept this observation to myself.

Upon returning to Bhopal, we revisited the hospital early the next morning. I was sure that I had uncovered some clues against Mumtaz. I smelt his hands again, from which the odour of gunpowder still emanated. I called the medico-legal team immediately and asked them whether his hands were burnt because of some explosion or acid.

They said his hands had been burnt because of acid. However, when they smelt his hands, they also noticed the odour of gunpowder. They called the person who worked in the laboratory to Mumtaz's bed. He took a small piece of skin from his hand for examination. I went to the laboratory with the medico-legal team, and within a few minutes, they confirmed that there was a stench of acid as well as gunpowder coming from his hands.

This new evidence was significant. It suggested that Mumtaz had been involved in an explosion, which contradicted his statement about being attacked with acid. Additionally, the call records placing his associate in Gyaraspur at the time of the incident further corroborated this finding. We returned to the CID headquarters, where I called Maqshood, but he was not available at his residence. I called up the TI of Gyaraspur police station and asked him whether he had registered any case of robbery. He informed me that according to the kotwar's report, he had registered a case of attempt to commit dacoity against unknown culprits the previous night.

Because Mumtaz was still in a bad state, we couldn't grill him. However, we tried to quiz him by changing our team members. Though he was writhing in pain, he never deviated from his statement. We also came to know that Mumtaz had four to five accomplices, which became apparent after interviewing the villagers and the kotwar. With the help of the Noor Bagh police station, when we laid our hands on two of his chums and Maqshood, we brought them all to the CID office. Perhaps Maqshood realized that the police suspected him, so when we grilled him, he revealed a conspiracy that he and Mumtaz had concocted.

⁓

Maqshood finally admitted that he and Mumtaz, along with three others carrying hand grenades, had tried to loot a house in Gyaraspur area. However, the burglary went awry when one of the grenades exploded in Mumtaz's hands, causing severe injuries. As a result, they had to run away. The villagers did not see them, even though the sound of the explosion had woken them up. He then washed Mumtaz's hands with acid to lessen the impact of the burns and took him to a private health centre in Bhopal from where he was referred to Hamidia Hospital. To cover up the incident and shift the blame, they devised a plan to frame Ashudani for the attack.

As part of the plan, Mumtaz, in his statement, accused Ashudani's hired henchmen of forcing him to submerge his hands in a bucket of acid. Both of them thought that by appearing before the court as victims, they could extract a lot of money from the contractor. 'So, I told the Hamidia Hospital staff that the incident had taken place at Badi, where Ashudani was constructing a road. Because of my report, the hospital forwarded all the fabricated evidence, including Mumtaz's statement, the eyewitness' account, and the medical report, to the police station in Badi, leading to the registration of a case against Ashudani,' said Maqshood.

His story numbed us all for a while. I heaved a sigh of relief because we had finally solved a complicated case and saved an innocent person from unjust persecution.

7

Friend or Foe?

A wealthy businessman's son fell victim to a harrowing kidnapping plot orchestrated by associates of the notorious gangster Dawood Ibrahim.

It was high noon on a rainy day in 2005. The rain clouds were floating across the welkin, making the weather slightly clammy. I was seated in ADG (Intelligence) S.K. Rout's office at the police headquarters in Bhopal.

Rout was familiarizing me with Indore, where I had recently been posted as IG. I had left for Indore in a hurry and intended to return to Bhopal after Independence Day to meet some senior officers at the police headquarters. Rout was telling me about the importance of Indore, which, along with being a commercial centre, is politically sensitive. My phone rang in the middle of our conversation, breaking the cadence.

Adarsh Katiyar, SP Indore, was on the line. 'A Škoda car was found abandoned at Ralamandal near the Tejaji Nagar bypass under the Andha Kuan police station in Indore this morning. The car was facing towards Agra on the Agra–Bombay road. The Andha Kuan police searched the car and found a few empty packets of cigarettes and a half-full bottle of whisky. Three windowpanes of the car were closed, but the one beside the driver's seat was open. The door was locked and the key was nowhere to be found. Based on the papers found in the car, it came to light that the four-wheeler belonged to Mahesh, the owner of a cement factory in Pithampur and resident of Vishwanath Gali.

'When the police contacted Mahesh, they learned that his son, Hitesh Mahagori, had left for Hotel Valley View at 7.30 p.m. yesterday in that car to attend a friend's birthday party. He was accompanied by his friend, Aman Mohan. Mahesh Mahagori and his family members searched for Hitesh and Aman, but when they could not find the duo, they lodged a missing person's complaint at the police station. It was then obvious that Mahagori and his friend were missing.

'Hitesh belongs to a wealthy family. His family learnt from his other friends that both the youths were last seen at the bowling club in Hotel Evening Palace.'

After I heard Katiyar's narrative, I detected something suspicious in his account. 'I'm leaving the police headquarters shortly and will reach Ralamandal, where the car has been found. I will inform you about my arrival after reaching Dewas,' I told him. I also advised him, 'You should visit the site with the local police. We will meet Hitesh's and Aman's family members after visiting the spot.' While I was talking to Katiyar, it occurred to me that someone may have kidnapped the youths for ransom. It was possible because Indore is the business capital of Madhya Pradesh and many rich people live there. Several businessmen had been kidnapped from the city previously.

As I spoke with Katiyar, I noticed Rout observing me. Once I put down the receiver, he inquired if there was something significant, so I recounted the tale Katiyar had related to me.

I said, 'It may have been an incident of kidnapping for ransom.'

Rout, an experienced officer familiar with the topography and behaviours of the people of Indore, immediately said, 'There should not be any suspicion. It is indeed a case of kidnapping for ransom. It cannot be anything else.'

He also told me that the press and residents of Indore were very sensitive to such incidents.

'Your ordeal begins now,' Rout remarked. 'Rush to Indore and meet the DGP to discuss the case with him.'

'I am sending the IG of Indore to you to discuss a kidnapping case and then you can inform the chief minister about it,' Rout told DGP Puri over the intercom.

I entered the DGP's chamber and noticed that a few officers were with him. It appeared that he had been awaiting my arrival, as he promptly sought feedback on the incident. He advised me to proceed to the location and expressed satisfaction that I was taking the case seriously. He also said, 'Gentleman, your difficult times start now. Keep me posted about the incident.'

I immediately set out from Bhopal for Indore by road. On the way, I discussed the incident with other police officers and tried to get as much information as possible.

I also received calls from my journalist acquaintances based in Indore. They told me, 'You are new to the city, and should the kidnapping be connected to ransom, it will be a turning point for your career. Your name will be remembered in Indore in relation to this case.'

By the time I entered Indore, evening was already setting in, with sunlight filtering through the clouds and casting a warm glow on the roadside trees.

I reached the spot and noticed Katiyar and his team waiting for me. Together with DIG Pramod Phadnikar, Katiyar, ASPs Rajesh Hingankar and Dharmendra Choudhary, City SP Arvind Tiwari and other officials, we examined the Škoda again but this time with a forensic laboratory officer. He had already taken fingerprints and other physical evidence from the car and tyre marks from the road.

Except for the empty cigarette packets and the half-full bottle of whisky, there was nothing much that we could lay our hands on. So we proceeded to the residence of Hitesh Mahagori. The Mahagoris were already present at the house because they knew I was going to visit them. I held a meeting with them collectively and then individually. However, nobody could come up with any explanation for Hitesh's sudden disappearance. We then went to Aman's house to speak to his family members. His mother abruptly mentioned receiving a call on the landline a few minutes ago, informing them that Aman was safe and not to worry about him.

According to her, the caller said, 'We have nothing to do with Aman. Our purpose is to keep Hitesh. As soon as our work is done, we will set him free.'

The phone had no caller ID, so it was impossible to identify the person. The telephone department also was unable to provide any leads. We spoke to the senior officials of the telephone department and arranged for caller ID installation on both Aman's and Hitesh's landline numbers.

We convened at the police control room to devise a strategy for further action. It was evident to us that Hitesh had been kidnapped for ransom, and Aman, being in his company, had also been abducted. Given Aman's modest background, his family lacked the means to pay a ransom.

Upon reaching my residence, I narrated the story to Additional DGP Rout over the phone, who also agreed that the youths had been kidnapped for ransom. I spoke to DGP Puri as well. He said, 'I have received several phone calls from Indore. The incident has kicked up dust in the city.' Following this, I phoned Katiyar and told him that given the call received at Aman's residence, we should register a case of kidnapping for ransom. Katiyar agreed and a case was then registered at the Ramganj police station.

The next morning, I discussed the case with the DIG (Indore), SP (Indore) and other police officers and decided to revisit the location. However, we could not find a clue to uncover the culprits. Similarly, our second visit to Hitesh's and Aman's residences proved fruitless. The caller ID had been installed and I advised both families to keep me posted about any developments regarding the incident.

Police officers in civilian clothes were posted outside both houses to keep us informed of any developments. After meeting the families, we went to Hotel Evening Palace, where we inspected the bowling club and spoke with the employees. One of them claimed to have seen a young man in the bowling club on the evening of the incident. Unfortunately, with no CCTV cameras in those days, we could not get any electronic evidence.

Returning to the police control room, we discussed the investigation's progress with the head of the Ramganj police station and set up a special investigation team. Police officers were sent to Delhi, Mumbai, Patna and Lucknow because in previous kidnapping cases, the abductors' links had been found in these cities.

Nearly three days had passed since Hitesh was kidnapped, but his family received no ransom call. We held meetings every morning and evening and were constantly connected with the teams sent to Delhi, Mumbai, Patna and Lucknow.

However, it felt like we were missing a crucial clue. The team sent to Mumbai reported that a similar kidnapping had occurred in Pune, where a young individual had been abducted, although the gang responsible remained unidentified. A ransom demand of ₹2 crore had been made in that case.

Days passed with no information regarding Hitesh and Aman, and we found ourselves unable to provide answers to the mounting questions from both the police headquarters and the press, who were quick to highlight our perceived inefficiencies.

After about a week, the Mahagoris received a call. Hitesh's sister answered the phone, and the police officers deployed outside her house informed me about it.

'Hitesh is with us,' informed the caller. 'Arrange for ₹4 crore within two days. Do not act smart. Otherwise, you will get Hitesh's body in pieces.'

I spoke to the sister and noted the phone number on the caller ID. When we contacted the telephone department, we discovered that it was an international call from Jeddah, Saudi Arabia.

The call made it clear that the kidnapping had an international connection. It scared the Mahagoris so much that they contacted tantriks (witchcraft practitioners) and godmen and prayed in temples for Hitesh's protection. They also met a spiritual saint of Indore, who advised them to perform witchcraft to dispose of the problem, and they obeyed the order. We, however, ignored all that and continued to do our work.

The date for paying the ransom was fast approaching. We knew that call was from Jeddah but we didn't know the caller's identity. Our attempts to seek assistance from the Indian High Commission in Jeddah through Interpol yielded limited results due to bureaucratic delays and the slow pace of the Saudi Arabian home ministry's response. We could not send any reminder to our earlier letter within 15 days because of the protocol between India and Saudi Arabia.

On the other hand, the press and residents of Indore directed their anger at the police department. Moreover, the police headquarters and administration were regularly seeking feedback on the case. The journalists were calling up the DGP frequently. Finally, we decided to plunge into action instead of counting on the slow system of the country and sent a person to Jeddah at our own expense to investigate the caller's identity.

Additionally, we shared the Jeddah phone number with our teams in Mumbai and Delhi, instructing them to coordinate with the respective crime branches to uncover any pertinent details regarding the call's origin and the identity of the caller.

There was no further communication from Jeddah, but the Mahagoris received a call from a local PCO. The caller instructed the family to deposit ₹10 lakh at ICICI Bank in a particular account number or else the kidnappers would kill Hitesh. We soon gathered information about the account holder from the ICICI Bank branch where the money was to be deposited. The account belonged to an individual named Ramesh Katju, a resident of Hira Sagar. We tried to contact the man but he seemed to be non-existent. According to the bank officials, the account had been opened through an agent. Therefore, the account holder's address had not been verified. Meanwhile, a token amount was deposited in the given account by the Mahagoris without our knowledge. The next day, we learnt that the money had been withdrawn from an ATM in Sanyogita Ganj using the same account number.

The security guard at the ATM was unable to provide any information about the person who had withdrawn the money. The Mahagoris kept receiving calls from different PCOs twice or thrice a day to deposit the remaining funds in the account. The individual visited the PCO either during the night or at daybreak and despite our efforts to pursue them, they consistently managed to leave the PCOs before our arrival.

We had deployed nearly 60 police officers outside a few PCOs. Because there were 400 PCOs in the area, it was not possible for us to watch each of them round the clock. We got details of the ATM card that was used to withdraw the money and had it blocked with the help of ICICI Bank. Watching the PCOs, however, came to nought because the kidnappers realized that the police were on the job. They also realized that if they tried to use a PCO, they would get caught.

✌

On the morning of 26 August, we received word that the body of a young man resembling Aman Mohan had been discovered in the Maksi area of Shajapur. A police team rushed to the spot, and as they were identifying the body, we waited with bated breath. I nervously paced in the police control room as I had to reply to the questions from the police headquarters. I heaved a sigh of relief after learning that it was not Aman's body. A local youth had been murdered and his body had been dumped there.

The Mahagoris received another call to keep ₹10 lakh ready. The caller said that he would inform about the drop location later. The call was traced with the help of the service provider and the caller was identified as Suresh Raikwar, a resident of Khategaon. He had used his motorcycle licence as a document to get the SIM card issued. We sent a team to Khategaon but discovered that the licence was forged. Nobody named Suresh Raikwar lived there. We failed again but did not give up.

Our cyber team traced the IMEI number of the caller's mobile device with the help of the mobile number and retrieved another number that was working on it. Tracing that number, the police reached Suthaliya and caught a PCO owner, who revealed that a person named Pandit had borrowed his phone for a while. Pandit had said that his phone's battery had drained and hence had asked for the PCO owner's mobile.

Based on the information provided by the PCO owner, a police team reached Pandit's residence and took him into custody. When questioned, he said that he had nothing to do with the kidnapping; after learning from the newspapers that a businessman's son had been kidnapped, Pandit had also wanted to make some money, so he had made the call asking for ₹10 lakh. We arrested Pandit and his accomplice but were unable to catch the real culprits. This left us frustrated and on edge, with the investigation leading nowhere.

Sometime later, I received a call from Rout, who advised me not to go beyond Indore to search for the culprits. I was told that a special task force (STF) of the police headquarters would handle operations outside Indore, as an international gang was involved in the crime.

'It is our responsibility to smoke the crooks out because the case has been registered in Indore. Besides, there is no James Bond in the STF to bring back the kidnapped person by plane to Indore without any fuss. We will keep away from the STF and will not call our teams back from Mumbai and Delhi. We will search every nook, and if need be, we shall continue our probe in foreign lands,' I replied to Rout. I did not know whether he liked my response. He said that he had been told to communicate the directive to me and that he did. 'You can have it your way,' Rout ended the call.

Perhaps he too was against keeping Indore Police away from the investigation.

In the meantime, our man in Jeddah returned to Indore, claiming to have found out the details of the subscriber of the phone number being used from there.

'The phone number belongs to Joseph, a cohort of Dawood Ibrahim, who runs a gang from Jeddah,' our man said. As there was no extradition treaty between India and Saudi Arabia then, Joseph could not be brought into the country.

Our hopes were shaken when we heard Dawood's name. I told my team members not to lose heart and continue working. However, we were certain that the chances of Hitesh being alive were higher. Big gangs rarely kill a kidnapped person because they only care about the ransom. In contrast, small gangs usually dispose of an abducted person after getting the ransom for fear of being arrested.

Our officer deputed to the Mumbai telephone gateway

uncovered that Joseph's gang had made two calls to mobile numbers in Delhi over the past six months, targeting affluent businessmen and extorting large sums of money as ransom. Both businessmen, threatened by the kidnappers, had paid ₹1 crore each to secure their safety.

Furthermore, we came to know that Joseph's gang had been behind the Pune kidnapping as well. I sent two teams to Pune and Mumbai to find out the links between the Mahagori case in Indore and the Gotia case in Pune.

While our teams were working everywhere in the country, the government and police headquarters continued to bombard me with questions. The media in Indore also continued their relentless scrutiny. It weighed heavily on me. I endured all that with courage and the support of my teammates, particularly the very cool-headed Adarsh Katiyar.

Meanwhile, the Mahagoris did not receive any call for ransom either from Jeddah or any other place for a couple of days.

Our team in Pune informed us that Vinod's body had been found near Surat.

The Gotias, desperate for proof of Vinod's well-being, were instructed by the kidnappers to retrieve a video cassette from a prominent Hanuman temple.

Despite their efforts, the Gotias failed to locate the tape at the temple when they went there with the cops. The kidnappers called the Gotias for the second time. Vinod's family informed them that they could not find any tape. The kidnappers then told the family that they had gone to the wrong place and gave them another address. The police suspected that someone who had accompanied the family to the temple was in touch with the kidnappers and that the same person had informed the kidnappers that they had reached the wrong location.

The police interrogated those who had accompanied Vinod's

family to the temple. As soon as the kidnappers came to know of the police's involvement, they killed Vinod and threw his body on the highway.

❧

Back in Indore, the abductors called the Mahagoris from Jeddah once again to demand ransom. We had trained Hitesh's sister to chat with the kidnappers for as long as possible and ask them to let her speak to her brother. When the kidnappers called, she began to wail over the phone, pleading to get proof that her brother was alive.

'A few fake gangs have also plunged into action for ransom. The members of that gang had learnt from the newspapers that my brother had been kidnapped, and they took money from us. Please let me talk to my brother,' she requested them.

However, the call abruptly ended. She received another call from Jeddah that evening.

The caller said, 'We are giving you one last chance. Tomorrow morning, we will let your brother talk to you. You will be given a code number to transfer ₹4 crore through hawala to Singapore, Tokyo or Karachi. Otherwise, your brother will be killed.'

Both my team and the police headquarters intercepted the call. The senior officers instructed the SP to advise the Mahagoris to pay the money to save Hitesh's life. The police would take care of the kidnappers later. When Adarsh informed me about the instructions given to him from the police headquarters, my reply to him was very abrupt: 'We are not obliged to follow anybody's advice in the investigation of a kidnapping case as long as the case is with us.' We did not comply with the order.

Our officer posted at the telephone gateway in Mumbai was tasked with monitoring all calls originating from the Jeddah landline number. The officer soon informed us that a phone call was made from Jeddah to a mobile number in Delhi. We alerted our Delhi team, which located the subscriber of that number with help from the Delhi crime branch.

Because the number was taken only two days ago, the name and address of its subscriber could not be verified as customer verification was done within one week after issuing the SIM card in those days. The crook was very smart. Except for this SIM, he had not used any other SIM card on the mobile equipment. Hence, no other mobile number could be found with that IMEI.

We were able to obtain a clue regarding the mobile's location, which was somewhere near Hudson Lane in Delhi. Having placed that number under interception, we soon found that there was another call from Jeddah on the same number.

The caller said, 'A man named Somesh will visit you in the morning. Your number is new, so it is not under police surveillance; hence, you will give this phone to Somesh who will help Hitesh talk to his sister through this phone. She will send the ransom through hawala. If the money is not transferred by tomorrow evening, we will close the case as we did in Pune.'

Upon receiving this information from the Delhi team, I realized that I was at an impasse with no tangible leads, and I lamented my decision to withhold Hitesh's family from paying the ransom despite clear advice from the higher-ups to let the Mahagoris hand over the money to the kidnappers. I was confident that the people of Madhya Pradesh would narrate the story of my failure to everyone. It seemed like only God could help us now. My prayers were heard, and what happened next was a miracle.

The man who had been using the mobile phone and was to hand it over to Somesh the next morning inserted his own SIM card into the new phone. As soon as he did that, we tracked his number through the IMEI number of the mobile device with the help of the Delhi crime branch. The number belonged to a felon named Maninder Singh 'Jagga'. This lead breathed new life into our team members.

With the help of Delhi Police, we arrested Maninder from a food outlet. The SIM card was confiscated from him. He had called to inform his wife that he would not be able to return home at night due to some important work. His phone battery had died and he could not complete his conversation with his wife, so in a hurry, he put his personal SIM card without much thought. When questioned, Jagga said that he was supposed to give the SIM card to Somesh at ISBT (Inter-State Bus Terminus) at 5 a.m. the next morning.

'Take Somesh into custody as soon as he reaches ISBT in the morning, but take all the necessary precautions,' I instructed my team in Delhi.

When Somesh neared ISBT the next day, Jagga gave our team a signal, who, with the help of the Delhi crime branch, pinned him down. The news of Somesh's arrest took the edge off me. During his interrogation, we realized that Somesh was a tough nut to crack; he refused to divulge any information about the whereabouts of the abducted youths.

I instructed City SP Dilip Soni and TI B.S. Parihar to take both the crooks to the Agra–Bombay highway and question them at gunpoint. I also told them that if required, they should threaten them with dire consequences.

When City SP Soni placed the barrel of his pistol into Somesh's mouth, he surrendered and revealed crucial details. He said that Hitesh and Aman were being held near a bypass in Guna district, on the border of Madhya Pradesh and Rajasthan. We enlisted the help of J.P. Pali, an underworld expert and ASP posted in Neemuch. Immediately after getting my call, he came to our aid in Indore.

Subsequent investigation revealed that Aman had a friend

named Roshan who ran a tailoring shop in Shivpuri. Even before the kidnapping, many of Aman's acquaintances had seen Roshan in Indore. I sent Pali to Shivpuri to inquire about Roshan, who was not at home. In Shivpuri, we were told that Roshan had attended the wedding of Dawood's daughter in Dubai. Roshan had sewn the bridal outfit that Dawood's daughter Mahrukh wore when she tied the knot with Javed Miandad's son Junaid. Roshan himself took the wedding attire to Dubai.

I instructed Soni and Parihar to rush to Guna with Somesh and Jagga and told Pali to proceed to Guna from Shivpuri as reinforcement. Both the teams reached Guna at almost the same time.

They successfully found the hutment where the youths had been held captive and rescued them. Two outlaws, Abdul and Razzak, armed with pistols, kept an eye on the kidnapped youths round the clock. The police also took Abdul and Razzak into custody.

Upon interrogation, it came to light that Somesh was Roshan's agent. On Roshan's insistence, Somesh had joined Dawood's gang. It also came to light that Dawood himself had told Roshan, 'If you do something big, you will get ₹1 crore as a gift for stitching the bridal outfit.'

That is the reason why Roshan had organized Hitesh's abduction.

With both youths safe and four criminals in our custody, we finally relaxed after a fortnight of what clearly was an immensely gruelling ordeal.

❧

Our team left for Indore with the accused, and I instructed them to question the suspects along the way. Given the high-profile nature of the case, I anticipated media scrutiny, making it challenging to be tough on such hardened criminals. Thus, the team stopped the vehicles en route and questioned Abdul and Razzak. This revealed a turn that we had not anticipated.

Abdul and Razzak indirectly hinted that they were mere pawns and the real mastermind was someone else. When Inspector Parihar pressed them for details, what they revealed was truly shocking: Aman and his friend, Rakesh, were the masterminds behind Hitesh's kidnapping.

Rakesh and Aman had studied together in the same school. Hoping to earn a huge amount of money in one go, Aman and Roshan kidnapped Hitesh. Aman, who had appeared to be a victim, had actually played a key role in orchestrating Hitesh's kidnapping. Rakesh had been a covert partner in the kidnapping conspiracy.

Thus, in a startling turn of events, the investigation into this case unveiled a complex web of deceit and betrayal. What initially appeared to be a case of a wealthy businessman's son falling victim to a kidnapping plot orchestrated by associates of a notorious gangster took an unexpected twist. Aman, who had seemingly been a victim, turned out to be the mastermind of the entire scheme, with Rakesh as his covert partner. As the truth emerged, justice prevailed and the abducted youths were rescued. The case serves as a reminder of the complexity of criminal investigations and the importance of thorough examination to uncover the truth.

8

Tête-à-Tête with Mumbai's Underbelly

Veiled in secrecy, Mumbai's treacherous underbelly conceals many clandestine dealings. Their notorious exploits, entangled in a web of betrayal and rivalry, paint a vivid picture of the city's criminal landscape.

esides Dawood Ibrahim, another notorious underworld kingpin is Chhota Rajan. In 2004, a member of Chhota Rajan's gang, Vicky Malhotra, made a call from Bangkok to a liquor baron in Indore, demanding ₹4 crore from him. Chhota Rajan alleged that the liquor baron had earned a lot of money by peddling opium.

Vicky Malhotra told the liquor baron that he would get abducted if he did not comply. Scared, the trader contacted the police in Indore and relayed his ordeal. The trader also shared the mobile number from which he had received the call. The police registered a case but failed to grasp the significance of the mobile number. Indore's police officers had links with some of their counterparts in Mumbai. They shared the number with officers in the Mumbai Police crime branch, who placed the number under surveillance.

In 2005, Dawood Ibrahim arranged the wedding of his daughter Mahrukh to former Pakistani cricketer Javed Miandad's son Junaid. While Dawood was preparing for his daughter's wedding, Vicky came to India on a secret mission. As soon as Vicky arrived at Mumbai airport, he unknowingly activated the same number used to demand money from the liquor baron in Indore, alerting the Mumbai police. Vicky reached the national capital by the next flight, where amidst rapidly changing circumstances, he was arrested by Mumbai police.

Around this time, I was posted to Indore as IG. When I came to know about Vicky Malhotra's arrest, I reopened the case of the ransom threat to the liquor baron. With a production warrant from the court, I brought Vicky to Indore.

The Human Rights Commission decreed that a criminal's

health would be examined in the morning and evening and that he was to be questioned only in the presence of his lawyer. Vicky, fearing strict treatment from the Indore police, submitted applications to the National Human Rights Commission, State Human Rights Commission and various courts to prevent the use of any third-degree methods. The police, however, did not treat him as a criminal and sought to establish a friendly rapport with him.

I went to the police station, offered a chair to Vicky and asked whether he would like to have breakfast. My behaviour took him by surprise. Vicky, his advocate and I shared tea and samosas. I took his lawyer into confidence and assured him that our objective was not to harass Vicky but to extract some information about Dawood from him.

I told Vicky to rest and sent his lawyer to a hotel. I told everyone to take care of Vicky's security and arrange for proper food for him at the police station.

I went to the police station again in the evening, called Vicky to my chamber and said, 'What would you like to eat?'

He said, 'I'm a vegetarian and fond of idli.'

I said, 'Would you like to have drinks?'

He said, 'I take only non-alcoholic drinks. I'm fond of thandai.'

I then asked him about his family. He said he had a wife and a son. I further asked him whether he would like to talk to them.

He said, 'Yes.'

I arranged for a private phone call between Vicky and his family members. I told him that if he wanted to meet his wife, she could be called to Indore. He readily agreed to my proposal. I arrsanged for his wife and son to be brought to Indore. At night, I got a call from the TI who was taking care of Vicky's security. He informed me that Vicky wanted to meet me.

On reaching the police station, I invited Vicky to join me on the sofa. As we sat down and enjoyed our tea, an unexpected wave of emotion overcame Vicky. Suddenly, he rested his head on my shoulder and tears began streaming down his face.

I encouraged Vicky to recount his journey and delve into the intricate web of crime in which he was entangled. Due to our warm treatment, Vicky felt at ease and peeled the layers of his life, sharing the darker aspects and complex operations he had participated in.

What struck me most was Vicky's meticulous attention to detail. His narrations were incredibly thorough as he recounted his journey into the underworld with astonishing clarity. He recalled every minute detail, including precise dates and times, demonstrating extraordinary memory for each incident. It was fascinating to witness his openness and willingness to share the workings of his operations, as well as the intricate details regarding the origins and functioning of various infamous underworld characters.

⤜❦⤛

Vicky revealed that his real name was Vijay Kumar Yadav and that he was a resident of Murshidabad district in West Bengal. He began committing petty crimes in his childhood, before eventually moving to Mumbai due to financial struggles. Vicky said that one day, after stealing diamonds from a jewellery shop, he saw Shah Rukh Khan's film *Baazigar* with his associates. In the film, the actor's name was Vicky Malhotra, so his friends changed his name from Vijay Kumar Yadav to Vicky Malhotra.

Neither his wife nor the other members of his family knew what Vicky was doing in Mumbai. He had told his family members that he dealt with readymade garments and that he used to export cloth from Mumbai to Nepal and Bangladesh. His real story came to light after he was arrested in Delhi and the news was telecast on every television channel. His wife and relatives then learnt that the person known as Vicky Malhotra was their Vijay Kumar Yadav.

While he did start his career in Mumbai as a cloth supplier, he was discontent with his modest earnings. When Vicky entered the underworld, he met Chhota Rajan—'Nana' to his gang members—and became one of his close aides.

The relationship between Chhota Rajan and Dawood was not always bad. Both used to work together for the Mumbai underworld but their relationship soured following the 1993 Mumbai bombings. They used to make a huge amount of money by betting on cricket, usurping disputed properties, peddling drugs, supplying arms and fake currency notes and kidnapping people for ransom. Both used to give a huge amount of brass to a few politicians, some detective agencies as well as local authorities. However, the fallout in 1993 led to intense rivalries and frequent clashes between the two gangs. Dawood targeted many people by triggering the blasts and then fled India.

After leaving India, Dawood relocated to Pakistan, where he remained under the ISI's protection. From Pakistan, Dawood continued to incite violence in India and extort money through his aides. Meanwhile, Chhota Rajan also left India, initially residing in Malaysia before going into hiding in Bangkok. One day, when Chhota Rajan was in an apartment in Bangkok, Munna Jhingra and his acolytes attacked him. They first shot Chhota Rajan's caretaker, Rohit Verma, who had opened the door. The attackers then murdered Rohit's wife, Sangeeta, their daughter and a female domestic worker.

Chhota Rajan hid in one of the bedrooms in the apartment before escaping through a window. The raiders searched for him but could not find him anywhere, so they fired at the bedroom door that was locked. Though the raiders did not find anyone in the room, they kept firing blindly. Munna Jhingra, who was leading the marauders, eventually realized that Chhota Rajan had slipped out of the window. The moment Vicky came to know about the incident, he called the police, who saw Chhota Rajan hanging from the branch of a tree behind his flat. He was brought down from there and sent to Samitivej Hospital, where Vicky remained by his side.

Since Chhota Rajan was admitted to the hospital under the pseudonym Vijay Daman, rumours began spreading that he had been killed in Bangkok. However, his true identity could not remain concealed for long, and Indian law enforcement agencies soon learnt that Chhota Rajan was receiving treatment in a hospital in Bangkok.

Vicky decided to enlist the help of the hospital employees and security staff by taking them into confidence. In the meantime, he visited India and carried a mannequin of Chhota Rajan in a big suitcase. Vicky said that he carried the upper part of the replica on the first visit and the lower part on the second. He also procured a long rope.

Because of Vicky's contacts in the hospital, Chhota Rajan was recovering well. However, as the Government of India issued an order for Chhota Rajan's extradition and a team of Central Bureau of Investigation (CBI) sleuths prepared to depart for Bangkok to apprehend him, Vicky swiftly sprang into action upon learning of their intentions through television channels.

He joined the two parts of the mannequin, put it on Chhota Rajan's bed and covered it with a bedsheet. Afterwards, Vicky helped Chhota Rajan slip away through the window using the rope and escorted him to a car to escape from the hospital. Vicky told the hospital staff that Nana was sleeping, so he should not be disturbed. When a nurse went inside the room to give Chhota Rajan medicine, she instead found the mannequin and the CBI team had to return from Bangkok empty-handed.

When Dawood's daughter died of jaundice, efforts were made to assassinate him during her burial. For this mission, Vicky left Kathmandu for Karachi with a Nepalese passport and stayed in a hotel with an associate. He bought two AK-47 rifles from an arms peddler and planned to go to the burial ground where Dawood's daughter was to be laid to rest to finish Dawood. Unfortunately, the ISI sleuths caught the arms smuggler who admitted to selling two AK-47 rifles to two Nepali boys. Immediately thereafter, the ISI informed Dawood about it. As a result, Dawood did not go to the burial ground. Vicky and his accomplice reached the burial ground only to realize that security had been heightened and Dawood was nowhere in sight. They threw away their rifles and navigated their way through the inaccessible terrains of Baluchistan to reach Afghanistan.

Luck favoured Dawood again in Dubai, where yet another plan to eliminate him had been devised. Dawood was a regular visitor to the India Club in Dubai, which was accessible only to individuals with properties worth ₹1,000 crore or more. Here, Dawood's agent, Danny (also known as Sharad Shetty), would announce gold rates in the morning, influencing global markets and thereby giving Dawood control over gold rates.

This time, Vicky and his accomplice reached Nepal using Bangladeshi passports, from where they went to Karachi. They bought two AK-47 rifles, two pistols and two LED TV sets. Concealing the firearms within the TVs, they sealed them using adhesive glue on the screws.

Vicky bought a ship worth ₹60 crore and set out for Dubai by sea with the TV sets containing the guns. Renting an apartment in a 56-storey building next to the India Club, Vicky and his accomplice began living there, waiting for Dawood. But as luck would have it, Dawood didn't show up for a visit for several months. The Dubai police, suspicious of Vicky and his accomplice, searched their apartment but couldn't find any incriminating evidence.

The police did try to open the TV sets but were unable to do so because of the glued screws. After their visit, Vicky was sure that he was on the radar of the Dubai police and Dawood. Instead of waiting for Dawood, Vicky took out the firearms from within the TV sets, raided the India Club, shot Sharad Shetty and left Dubai.

❧

While Vicky narrated his experiences, we fulfilled his request of calling his wife and son to Indore. The police ensured the safety and well-being of his family members to the best of their ability. Vicky's family stayed in Indore for seven days and then left for home under police protection. In return, Vicky said that he would provide me with all of Dawood's contacts in Madhya Pradesh. Using the information provided by Vicky, I set a trap to catch Dawood's agents operating in the state, and for this, I took the higher authorities into confidence. However, before I could execute my plan, I was transferred from Indore to Bhopal.

❧

Dawood Ibrahim's journey from a troubled youth in the lanes of Mumbai to India's most wanted criminal is marked by a trail of violence and deceit. He was born in Ratnagiri district of Maharashtra on 27 December 1955. Dawood's father, Sheikh

Ibrahim Ali Kaskar, served as a constable in the Mumbai Police. When Dawood was in school, he fell into bad company and committed theft, robberies and smuggling. To prevent him from committing crimes, his father got him married to a girl named Zarina, but the marriage failed to keep him away from unlawful activities.

When Dawood was entering the underworld, a crook named Karim Lala was reigning supreme. Dawood began working for him and quickly earned notoriety in the criminal world in the 1980s. By that time, he had collected so much money that he began investing in the film industry and gambling. It was during this period that he came across Chhota Rajan, and together, they began committing major crimes in India as well as abroad, becoming infamous in Dubai and Mumbai. The 1993 serial blasts in Mumbai that claimed 250 lives and injured 1,000 people were orchestrated by Dawood Ibrahim, specifically targeting the Hindu community, and resulted in widespread devastation and loss of innocent lives, exacerbating communal tension; this served as the catalyst that created a rift between him and Chhota Rajan, fracturing their criminal alliance.

Dawood fled from India and reached Pakistan, where the ISI provided him shelter, after evading the police of various Gulf countries. Since 1993, he has operated from Karachi, frequently changing his identity and appearance to evade capture.

Vicky divulged that Dawood changes his name according to the people he meets from various regions and has used at least 13 aliases. With passports to many countries—two belonging to Pakistan, one to the United Arab Emirates and another to Yemen, Dawood's influence transcends borders.

Despite his fugitive status, Dawood's familial ties remain intact. The gangster's family consists of his wife Maizabin Sheikh, one son Moin Nawaz and three daughters Mahrukh, Mehreen and Maria. His third daughter Maria died in 1998. Mahrukh was married to Javed Miandad's son while Mehreen married a Pakistani–American named Ayub. Moin married Saniya, the daughter of a London-based businessman.

Amidst the intrigue of his clandestine existence, Dawood's presence in popular culture is undeniable, with Bollywood often depicting characters inspired by him and other underworld figures in moves like *Black Friday, Shootout at Lokhandwala, Shootout at Wadala, D Company, Once Upon a Time in Mumbai Dobaara!* and *D-Day*.

Chhota Rajan's entry into the underworld was marked by a combination of circumstance and ambition. Born as Rajendra Sadashiv Nikalje, he became another name associated with Mumbai's underworld. He was born in 1959 in Chembur's Tilak Nagar area in Mumbai and had three siblings, including a sister. Rajendra grew up in a modest household and stopped going to school after the fifth grade, taking up odd jobs to supplement his family's income.

His criminal career began not from an alley in Mumbai but from outside a cinema hall. At the age of 20, he began selling movie tickets in black. One day, when he was peddling tickets outside Sahakar Plaza, a police team arrived at the spot and assaulted the ticket sellers. Rajendra also received a few blows during the lathi charge, which enraged him so much that he snatched a stick from one of the police officers and retaliated.

The police took him into custody, and after a few months, when he was released from prison on bail, many crooks had an eye on him because they wanted a person like Rajendra to work for their gangs. He then joined the gang of Rajan Nayak, also known as Bada Rajan, and took on the moniker 'Chhota Rajan'. The gang members used to call Chhota Rajan 'Nana'. He used to extort money from industrialists and builders in Mumbai.

Bada Rajan developed bad blood with the Pathan brothers. In 1982, the Pathan brothers silenced Bada Rajan outside a local court in Mumbai through Abdul Kunju, who was associated with them. Kunju and Bada Rajan had become sworn enemies after Kunju tied the knot with the latter's girlfriend. Following Bada Rajan's murder, Chhota Rajan took over the reins of his mentor's gang and resolved to eliminate Kunju who, upon learning of it, became so scared of the new lord of Mumbai's underworld that he went to a police station and surrendered before the law. Chhota Rajan stuck to his guns and attacked Kunju during 1983–84, but his plans to extinguish his enemy fell through. Dawood Ibrahim, impressed by Chhota Rajan's prowess, decided to form an alliance with him.

Immediately after joining hands with Dawood, Chhota Rajan eliminated Kunju on a cricket field. Another crook, Chhota Shakeel, joined Dawood's gang. Around 1987, Dawood began counting on Chhota Rajan so much that he sent the latter to look after his work in Dubai. Chhota Rajan's friendship with Dawood began to frustrate Chhota Shakeel.

Gradually, Chhota Rajan took control of more than 125 hotels in Mumbai under bogus names. This pinched Chhota Shakeel so much that he, with the help of two other gang members, Sharad Shetty and Sunil Rawat, riled Dawood against Chhota Rajan by planting suspicions about him in the mind of the gang's kingpin. They told Dawood that once Chhota Rajan becomes very powerful in Mumbai and Dubai, the latter would grab all his properties.

When Dawood Ibrahim's brother-in-law, Ismail Parkar, was allegedly murdered by members of Arun Gawli's gang, Dawood sought retribution. Initially entrusting Chhota Rajan with the task of eliminating Gawli's associates, Dawood later grew dissatisfied with Rajan's unsuccessful attempts. Subsequently, Chhota Shakeel took charge and executed a strike in Mumbai's Byculla area, dealing a severe blow to Gawli's network. This turn of events strained the relationship between Chhota Rajan and Dawood, leading to a significant rift between the two gangsters.

Amidst escalating tensions, Dawood threw a party in Dubai that Chhota Rajan was also going to attend. However, someone informed Rajan over the phone that there was a plan to kill him and advised him against going there. The phone call changed his mind, and instead of attending the party, he visited his contact directly. Within a few hours, arrangements were made to send Chhota Rajan to Malaysia via Kathmandu. From Malaysia, he went to Cambodia, then reached Indonesia and finally settled in Bangkok.

Though Dawood's plan to finish Chhota Rajan backfired, Chhota Shakeel was delighted because he had become his boss's right-hand man, whereas Chhota Rajan was playing hide-and-seek with Dawood. When Chhota Shakeel came to know of Rajan's location in 2000, he sent four sharpshooters to wipe him out, but Rajan managed to escape.

Rajan also tried to eliminate Dawood Ibrahim thrice, but success always eluded him. In 2010, the Bangkok police came to know of Chhota Rajan's plan from one of his old acquaintances, Bunty Pandey, with whom Chhota Rajan had attacked Dawood for the first time in 1998 and then again in 2000.

Meanwhile, Interpol issued a red corner notice for him. In 2015, Rajan fell into a police dragnet in Bali, Indonesia, and was charged with committing 70 crimes and sentenced to life imprisonment. The Indian police brought him to Delhi, from where he was sent to Tihar Jail.

While the names of gang kingpins such as Dawood Ibrahim and Chhota Rajan are widely recognized, only a few know about the characters operating behind the scenes and executing sinister plans for their bosses. One such figure is Vicky Malhotra, a trusted lieutenant within Chhota Rajan's empire, whose association with Rajan spanned over 20 years.

Chhota Rajan relied so much on Vicky that he handed over the responsibility for extorting money, drug peddling and real estate trade to him. Vicky was, in other words, Chhota Rajan's heir. Dawood Ibrahim and his henchmen made several unsuccessful attempts to create a rift between Vicky and Rajan but their relationship only strengthened over time. Vicky's loyalty was so steadfast that even when gangsters like Sharad Shetty and Ravi Pujari left Chhota Rajan, he never did.

In 2005, Vicky plotted a final attempt on Dawood's life but before he could carry out his plan, security agencies apprehended him and Farid Tanasha. Upon being released on bail in 2010, Vicky took care of Chhota Rajan's businesses in Dubai and South Africa, including the smuggling of diamonds.

A mobster named Bharat Nepali executed Tanasha in 2010. Enraged, Vicky eliminated Nepali a few months after Tanasha's murder.

The intricate web of alliances and betrayals within Mumbai's underworld is a testament to the volatile nature of power and loyalty. When Dawood and Chhota Rajan were friends, Sharad Shetty, also known as Danny due to his resemblance to Bollywood actor Danny Denzongpa, used to be close to the latter. When Chhota Rajan left Dawood's gang, Shetty stayed with Dawood. Later, Chhota Rajan and Shetty became sworn enemies, and the latter played an important role in the attack on Rajan in Bangkok.

Chhota Rajan, however, did not remain silent. He exacted revenge by executing Shetty at the India Club in Dubai.

Vicky disclosed that before neutralizing Shetty, they had kept an eye on his activities at the India Club. On the day of the attack, Vicky and one of his associates waited in a car outside the club while two others entered the club with pistols. Unaware of Vicky's sinister design, Shetty was playing cards at the club when the former's henchmen fired at him from close range. Both the shooters had been instructed to not leave even a single bullet in their pistols.

❦

Amidst these power plays, Munna Jhingra emerges as another character in the rivalry between Dawood Ibrahim and Chhota Rajan. Formerly a wanderer in Mumbai, Munna's fortune shifted when Dawood entrusted him with the crucial task of eliminating Chhota Rajan. Munna had long harboured the ambition to work for Dawood and hence grabbed this opportunity eagerly. Venturing to Dubai in 1999, Munna's journey took an intriguing turn as he was later summoned to Karachi through Nepal under the directives of Chhota Shakeel. Dispatched from Karachi to Bangkok, Munna capitalized on his sharpshooting skills to execute the mission of eliminating Chhota Rajan.

Rapidly establishing himself as a dependable confidant of Chhota Shakeel, Munna found himself entangled in a well-crafted scheme aimed at neutralizing Rajan, who had been a persistent threat to Dawood's interests in Bangkok. Munna rented a flat next to Chhota Rajan's and began living there as a Pakistani national named Mohammed Saleem. According to the plan, a team of 10 shooters knocked on the door of Chhota

Rajan's flat at 8.30 p.m. on 14 December 2000. They entered the apartment under the guise of pizza delivery men. As soon as Rohit Verma, who was living in Chhota Rajan's flat, opened the door, the killers riddled his body with bullets.

Though it was a well-orchestrated plan, Chhota Rajan had a narrow escape. The Thailand police took all the assailants into custody.

⚜

In the labyrinthine world of Mumbai's underbelly, these individuals stand as pillars of intrigue and betrayal, weaving a complex narrative of power, loyalty and vengeance. Each character has left an indelible mark with their infamous legacies.

9

Carnage Averted

A high-stakes situation developed in Dhar district, Madhya Pradesh, where the police had to strategically diffuse communal tension at Bhojshala by navigating the delicate balance between different religious beliefs.

Bhojshala, located in Dhar, Madhya Pradesh, was constructed during the reign of Raja Bhoja of the Paramara dynasty, who ruled from AD 1010 to AD 1055. The temple is known for its architecture and was a renowned centre of learning and philosophy during that era. Scholars from various parts of India and abroad flocked to Bhojshala to study the six schools of Hindu philosophy,[*] and it was considered one of the largest learning centres of its time. Even after the death of Raja Bhoja, the institution continued for 200 years. The king had installed an idol of Goddess Saraswati (Vagdevi) in this building, which stood on 84 artistic pillars. However, in 1857, a British officer took the statue to England, where it remains today.

In subsequent years, disputes arose between the Hindu and Muslim communities regarding the ownership and usage of Bhojshala. Hindus claim that Raja Bhoja built the monument as a temple of Goddess Saraswati, while Muslims say that they have been offering namaz at the site since the days of Raja Bhoja. They call it Jama Mosque and Kamal Maula Mosque. These claims led to frequent law and order issues, communal tensions and violent clashes. The police had to resort to lathi charge and open fire to control the frenzied mobs, which resulted in many deaths. The monument became a focal point of contention and drew attention from various stakeholders, including politicians, administrative officers, the media and the courts.

Recognizing the historical significance surrounding Bhojshala, the Archaeological Survey of India (ASI) designated it as a protected monument. This decision aimed to preserve the site and prevent conflicts. Coordination between the ASI, the custodian

---

*The six orthodox schools of philosophy, known as *shatdarshanas*, consist of *Vaishesika, Nyaya, Samkhya, Yoga, Purva Mimansa* and *Vedanta* or *Uttara Mimansa*. Developed over generations, these philosophies are attributed to sages Konada, Gotama, Kapila, Patanjali, Jaimini and Vyasa.

of the monument, and the state, responsible for law and order, became essential. However, complying with the many instructions from the ASI proved nearly impossible for the state from the perspective of public order. It became a trial for the state's law and order machinery, and maintaining law and order became an arduous task.

Earlier, Bhojshala was open only on Fridays and Basant Panchami. In 2003, the ASI issued an order to begin a new tradition where Hindus were allowed to worship every Tuesday and on Basant Panchami from sunrise till sunset, while Muslims were allowed to offer namaz on Fridays. Tourists were allowed to visit the site on the other five days by paying an entry fee. Initially, the order intensified tension in the area, and many people lost their lives in the communal clashes that followed. The situation gradually normalized, and people accepted the new tradition.

❧

On 3 February 2006, Hindus were to celebrate Basant Panchami—the fifth day of the full moon in the spring. It was also a Friday. Just a few days before the celebrations, Bhojshala became the focal point of communal tension again as the ASI's order put the state's law and order machinery to the test. For the first time in its history, the order allowed both puja and namaz to be performed on the same day at Bhojshala, posing a logistical challenge as both communities sought to carry out their religious rituals.

According to the order, Hindus were granted access from sunrise to 12.30 p.m. and from 3.30 p.m. to sunset. Muslims were allotted prayer time from 1 p.m. to 3 p.m. This implied that arrangements had to be made to vacate Hindus within half an hour, from 12.30 p.m. to 1 p.m., for Muslims to offer namaz. Then, within half an hour, between 3 p.m. and 3.30 p.m., Muslims would need to vacate the place so that Hindus could return to worship Goddess Saraswati till sunset. This intricate arrangement aimed to accommodate both communities to observe their religious practices on the same day.

There was enthusiasm among the Hindus, especially those living in the Malwa region and around Bhojshala. Hindu outfits administered oaths to the people, invoking the holy water of the Ganga kept in a pitcher, to ensure widespread participation in the worship of Goddess Saraswati on Basant Panchami. It was anticipated that around one lakh people would gather at the site for the occasion. Similarly, Muslims also resolved to offer namaz at the monument on that very day. Members of the Students Islamic Movement of India (SIMI) sent their men to each village, asking the people of their community to send two persons from each family to offer namaz at Bhojshala on Basant Panchami. We sent a report about the destructive activities of SIMI in Bhojshala to the state's Intelligence department and informed the same to the Intelligence Bureau (IB) officers deputed there. On 8 February 2006, after noticing the destructive role of SIMI, the Government of India banned SIMI for the third time.

The plan presented an extraordinary challenge as both communities were deeply invested in their respective worship plans and anticipated large gatherings. The police and administration found themselves in a precarious position of maintaining law and order while ensuring the religious sentiments of both communities were respected.

The then chief minister personally monitored the situation in Dhar. He instructed the police to devise a foolproof plan to maintain law and order and ensure the security of life and property of the common people. He assured that the government would provide all the resources necessary to execute the plan.

As IG of Indore at that time, it was my responsibility to maintain public peace. When the chief minister visited Indore a few days before Basant Panchami, he took me aside and said that I must act fairly to ensure absolute communal harmony and the rule of law. He asked the chief secretary and DGP to provide me with all the required resources. The chief secretary also called me to inform that the central government's instructions should be followed in letter and spirit and that the duty of each police officer was to protect the law and maintain public peace and tranquillity.

I organized many meetings, spot visits and route marches with the commissioner of Indore, DIG, Collector and SP, Dhar. I also established an operational command and control centre to monitor minute-to-minute developments and take immediate corrective measures. Efforts were made to encourage consensus between both communities so that the law and order situation remained under control and the central government's instructions were implemented, but attempts to get the religious leaders of both communities on board proved unsuccessful.

We proposed to the Muslim leaders to offer symbolic namaz at the Lal Mosque or Kamal Maula Mosque outside Bhojshala, but they refused. I contacted the Maulvis in Bhopal, Dhar and Indore and convinced them to work in public interest. They assured that the people of their community, who lived outside Dhar, would not go to Bhojshala to offer namaz.

The state government deputed a senior political executive (the minister in-charge of Dhar) for effective communication and coordination between people and administration. He also tried to convince the religious leaders of both communities, but neither were ready to compromise. However, the political executive's intervention ensured confidence and a feeling of security and safety among people, and facilitated better coordination in administration and resource mobilization.

Another challenge that arose was that the yajna could not be halted midway. Additionally, vibrant rangolis were created with flower petals, rice and kumkum and other flower and leaf decorations adorned the area in front of the oil painting of Goddess Saraswati. Removing the intricately designed rangolis would be an impossible task. Moreover, as the puja had to be resumed after the namaz, it became evident that removing the oil painting of the Goddess from the designated spot for namaz was also not feasible. The looming possibility of riots between the two communities appeared inevitable. Both communities utilized print and electronic media to urge their members to actively participate in their respective religious practices at Bhojshala on Basant Panchami. As the fear of riots hung in the air, families of daily-wage employees living in Dhar began leaving their houses in search of safer places near Indore.

In this precarious situation, I turned to my trusted friend Ateeque Ahmad, a fellow student of Banaras Hindu University. I discussed the complex dilemma posed by the ASI's order and sought his insights on how to accommodate the offering of namaz without disrupting the ongoing yajna and without compromising the sanctity of the oil painting of Goddess Saraswati. I discreetly shared his suggestions with my colleagues.

❧

On the day of Basant Panchami, the then chief secretary Rakesh Sahni called me in the morning. He wanted to know if the administration would be able to allow Muslims to offer namaz. I said that it should be possible. Sahni asked about the logistics, and after careful consideration, he decided to send DGP Swaraj Puri and additional chief secretary of the home department Satya Prakash by helicopter to monitor the situation.

I requested him not to do so because I had all the resources required to deal with any problems that may arise. All the officials of the Indore division had been assigned duties based on the commissioner's advice and my suggestions. I explained that sending a senior officer to Dhar at this moment would create confusion, and potentially add to the complications. Sahni trusted my judgement and immediately cancelled the plan.

After inspecting all the arrangements and briefing the officers deployed outside Bhojshala and the outer cordon surrounding the monument, I reached the sanctum sanctorum to find that Hindu devotees had already started the havan and puja. I had to cross the havan to go to the rooftop and oversee the arrangements. Being a follower of Sanatan Dharma, I was in a great dilemma as to whether I should join the prayer and put some sandalwood in the havan kund or focus solely on my work. However, knowing that the day would be incredibly challenging, I chose to invoke the blessings of Goddess Saraswati by clasping my hands in reverence after taking off my belt, cap and shoes and placing them on the ground. I fervently prayed for fortitude to discharge my responsibilities amidst the testing circumstances and safeguard the region from communal discord. Additionally, I was also concerned about the careers of other senior officers who had tirelessly worked with me round-the-clock for over a fortnight. A minor mistake could damage their careers as well. As I oversaw all the decisions, I felt morally accountable for any mishap.

❧

Hindus had begun entering Bhojshala at daybreak. They came in thousands, from all directions, singing devotional songs and dancing to music. Many people from the minority community had also started gathering in various parts of the city. As the sun rose in the sky, the atmosphere became charged and tensions escalated. The number of people kept increasing, and the situation started getting out of control. Members of both communities stood separately on both sides of the roads throughout the town. Shops remained shut and the doors of every house were bolted from the inside. An uneasy calm hung over Dhar.

The residents, haunted by bitter experiences of past communal clashes, when many innocent lives were lost and properties were damaged, remained glued to their TV sets, watching the situation unfold. Electronic and print media representatives were present inside Bhojshala to witness both the communities offering prayers to their gods. It was a sea of humanity, but the police officers on duty remained unruffled.

We had made plans to maintain peace. Some tall and sturdy police officials (mostly wrestlers from the police department) clad in saffron gamchha were deployed in the temple's sanctum sanctorum, chanting slogans of 'Jai Shri Ram' (Victory to Lord Rama). Until 11 a.m., we allowed Hindus to enter the temple. However, I realized that the number of people was so great that any coercive action by the police would result in a stampede and many lives would be lost. I instructed the police officers to stop the entry of devotees from the outskirts of Dhar, and eventually, around noon, all entry gates of Bhojshala were closed.

When the police began stopping Hindus outside Bhojshala's main gate, the mob started throwing stones at the cops; it also damaged the vans of the media people. A stone hit DIG Madhu Babu on the chest, causing him to slump to the ground, but he quickly got up and continued leading his team. DIG Vipin Maheshwari, in charge of the internal affairs of Bhojshala, and DC Sagar, in charge of the sanctum sanctorum and conducting puja and namaz, were instructed to carry out evacuation plans.

We took all the necessary precautions to ensure that the

situation would not spiral out of control, basing our arrangements on the recommendations of judicial commission reports on various grave communal clashes that had resulted in major public disorders and caused loss of public life and property to a great extent.

Looking at the volatile and aggressive mood of the devotees inside Bhojshala, we realized that we would have to expel them from the monument. Hence, we requested the political executive to leave the Bhojshala premises because using force in his presence would be inappropriate. The senior leader understood our problem and gave us a free hand to deal with the situation.

At our request, the local Muslim head had issued oral instructions that only locals would offer namaz inside the monument, and not outsiders. However, even the local participants were in the thousands. Nonetheless, according to our secret plan, we prepared for 50 Muslims to offer namaz on the rooftop. This plan was based on the advice of my friend Ahmad, who said that in case of a large crowd, the Muslims could offer namaz on the rooftop of a mosque, in its corridor and even outside it. He also emphasized that namaz could not be offered in front of the oil painting of Goddess Saraswati or before any symbol of another religion and that there should be a mimbar (raised platform used by the preacher in a mosque) on the rooftop to offer namaz.

We had prepared a contingency plan accordingly. I had instructed a senior police officer to hide 50 Muslims in the residential area of the Bhojshala campus from early morning and bring them to the Bhojshala rooftop at the time of namaz.

The morning slowly transitioned into noon, and with each passing minute, a sense of unease settled over me as it became increasingly apparent that we would not be able to oust the Hindu devotees by 12.30 p.m. We then decided to move them out through the rear door of the monument.

Our saffron-clad police officers started pushing the teeming mob through the rear entry of Bhojshala while raising slogans of 'Jai Shri Ram'. The Hindu devotees failed to understand how the saffron towel-clad men had entered the sanctum sanctorum in the first place and why they were behaving in such a manner. In this way, we somehow managed to empty the sanctum sanctorum. A few antisocial elements, who always exploit such crucial situations, tried to set ablaze some vehicles and shops outside Bhojshala. This kind of behaviour always causes suffering for the common people on the streets. Observing the situation outside Bhojshala, I instructed the officers to employ the necessary force to uphold peace and public order, taking full responsibility for the decision. This declaration bolstered the morale of the officers, prompting them to work courageously and resolutely. I also advised the administration to impose a citywide curfew. With the sanctum sanctorum now vacated, the pivotal moment had come to implement our strategy of leading 50 Muslims to the rooftop for namaz. However, to my utter disappointment, the officer responsible for the task informed me that he had forgotten to carry it out. It became evident that our plan had been compromised, possibly due to a local officer or one of his associates leaking information to radical groups with the aim of thwarting our covert strategy to resolve the tense situation. Due to the unavailability of 50 Muslims to offer namaz, an officer suggested that Muslim officers should be asked to wear kurta–pyajama and offer namaz instead.

Meanwhile, I received a call from the chief secretary. 'It's 2.15 pm. Has namaz been offered?' he asked. I informed him that the city was under curfew and that the namaz was yet to begin. My response seemed to shock the senior officers at the Ministry. Perhaps the chief secretary was taken aback because he had trusted me by giving me free rein to handle the situation and cancelled the DGP and home secretary's visit based on my recommendation. I had failed to live up to his trust, and it was clear that he would soon take action against me and my team. He abruptly ended the call.

Despite efforts to prevent entry, a group of Muslims managed to reach the Lakkadpeetha area (near the rear side of Bhojshala), approximately 1 km from the premises. Police attempted to drive them away because there was a clear instruction that nobody would be allowed to enter the premises and a curfew had been imposed in the area. SP Asha Mathur sought permission to forcibly disperse them, even at the risk of her own life. On the one hand, there were thousands of Hindus, and on the other, there were Muslims in equal numbers. Asha Mathur, along with an armed police contingent, stood firm between them and displayed extraordinary bravery at a time when a small mistake could have resulted in bloodshed.

This turned out to be a stroke of divine grace. We received a message that some members of the minority community from this gathering were present with the Naib Kazi near Bhojshala. It immediately prompted us to change our strategy. I instructed DIG Pramod Phadnikar and SP D.C. Sagar to form a corridor with the help of a strong police contingent and bring the Naib Kazi and about a dozen Muslims to the rooftop of Bhojshala. They executed the task and successfully escorted the Naib Kazi and 13 Muslims to the rooftop through the main gate.

By the time the azan began, the February sun was slowly descending in the western sky. The melodic words of the azan filled Bhojshala. Numerous TV channels conducted live telecasts of the event. My team breathed a sigh of relief, and I expressed gratitude to God for accepting my morning prayers.

Meanwhile, I received a call from Additional DGP of Intelligence S.K. Rout, who wanted to know the reason why namaz was not being offered and conveyed the state government's displeasure and annoyance. I reassured him that all was well and that namaz had been offered. He seemed relieved. I also informed the chief secretary and senior political executive about the situation. The state government instructed us to lift the curfew immediately and restart the puja and yajna to further ease the tension in the area.

All those who offered namaz were escorted back to their respective homes in police vehicles, and the curfew was lifted. Immediately after the namaz, we announced through loudspeakers in the city that puja and yajna had commenced. People who were previously prevented from entering the monument premises were now allowed inside. As the puja and yajna began, Sanskrit shlokas reverberated throughout Bhojshala as the evening shadows descended upon the ancient monument.

The successful outcome was a result of the efficient work of the police, district administration and peace-loving people from both communities as well as the strong determination of the state government to establish the rule of law in Madhya Pradesh at any cost.

10

Swindlers Destroy Students' Futures

Several corrupt officers orchestrated a devastating blow to the aspirations of numerous students by exploiting the information technology system and the Right to Information Act. By creating loopholes within the system of the Madhya Pradesh Professional Examination Board, they shamelessly extorted significant sums of money. Tragically, countless students from middle-class backgrounds, driven by dreams of securing government jobs or gaining admission to esteemed medical and professional colleges, fell victim to this corrupt scheme.

On a serene morning during the rainy season, as I sat in my office, an unexpected encounter brought to light a corrupt scheme within the Madhya Pradesh Professional Examination Board, commonly known as Vyapam (an abbreviation of its Hindi name Madhya Pradesh Vyavsayik Pariksha Mandal). Head Constable Kumher Singh Tomar from Sagar district, accompanied by his relative Raghvendra Singh Sikarwar, stood before me. I recognized Tomar from my time as SP in Sagar, as he had served as my driver.

Tomar approached me and disclosed, 'Vyapam is scheduled to conduct a test for the recruitment of junior data entry operators soon. However, aspirants are being asked to pay ₹2 lakh. The aspiring candidate must hand over their original intermediate examination mark sheet along with ₹25,000 to an agent who is affiliated with the board officials. Following the examination, the candidate must pay an additional ₹75,000, with the remaining balance due once the results are declared. The candidates will receive their original mark sheet back only after they have paid the total amount of ₹2 lakh.'

<hr>

Raghvendra Sikarwar, Tomar's relative, had been contacted by a group of individuals involved in these illicit activities. Upon hearing Sikarwar's account, Tomar brought him to me, seeking assistance in apprehending the gang members. Realizing the gravity of the situation and convinced that a nefarious group was orchestrating these fraudulent recruitments, I immediately took charge of the case. To gather evidence, I obtained the phone number of the individuals who had contacted Sikarwar and proceeded to meet with DGP S.K. Rout. Accompanied by Tomar and Sikarwar, I presented the case details to him. Though Rout comprehended the extent of corruption within the recruitment board, we could not take immediate action due to a lack of concrete evidence.

It was decided that the police department's informer fund would provide Sikarwar with ₹25,000, which he would then hand over to the gang along with his Class 12 mark sheet. To gather further evidence, we initiated the interception of the phone numbers obtained from Sikarwar, which enabled us to eavesdrop on the conversations held by the users. Through these intercepted calls, we discovered that the gang involved in the board's recruitment process had summoned over 100 candidates to Bhopal a day before the examination. As we continued monitoring Sikarwar's discussions with the gang members, we gained insight into their illegal activities.

Meanwhile, I set up a special team led by ASP Ruchi Vardhan. A few officials of the Special Task Force were also included in the team. When Sikarwar arrived in Bhopal, a police team was already waiting at the Habibganj railway station for surveillance. They began tailing the gang members, who had come to receive Sikarwar and the other applicants, in private cars as soon as they left the railway station with all applicants. Tomar was also secretly following the recruitment agents in a separate car.

Before leaving the railway station, the gang members collected the candidates' mobile phones and switched them off. They also switched off their own phones. The cavalcade of agents went to Van Vihar and held some discussions with the candidates there. As their phones were switched off, it was difficult to intercept their calls, but it became evident that the candidates were being taken to different places in the city by the gang members.

The police continued to follow them. It was 8 p.m. when a few more cars were spotted. The motorcade comprising eight cars reached a place near Barkatullah University from where they seemed to suddenly vanish into thin air. The police officers chasing the agents stood flummoxed.

Tomar, however, was continuously trailing the swindlers. He saw some kind of activity going on when the cars reached a school in Baloda, which he then informed me about. I passed on the information to Ruchi Vardhan. By the time I finished talking to Ruchi, her team had already surrounded the school from all sides.

On entering the school building, the police saw nearly 100 candidates receiving answers to the recruitment exam's questions from agents. The police seized the question papers and arrested the culprits. The operation involved nearly 50 police officers.

The team arrested eight individuals who were taken to Shahpura police station, where an FIR was lodged on behalf of one of the candidates. All the other candidates were made witnesses in the FIR. Some more people associated with the gang were taken into custody in Patna in Bihar and Bina in Madhya Pradesh, based on the information provided by the detainees.

When the police interrogated the agents, they revealed how they operated. They also confessed to contacting candidates and negotiating prices for specific job positions. Later, they would call the candidates to Bhopal and solve the question papers in a school the night before the examination. This ensured that when the candidates received the same questions on exam day, they could secure high scores and secure the job.

⁊

Following the seizure of the question paper, I promptly contacted the chairman of Vyapam, informing him about the police's possession of the question paper for the upcoming junior data entry operator's examination scheduled for the following morning. I urged him to compare the seized question paper with the one prepared by the Professional Examination Board, which was to be distributed among the candidates the next day.

'There is no provision for opening the question papers outside the designated examination centres. The packets containing the question papers can only be opened there. The police must wait until morning,' responded the chairman, citing protocol.

Undeterred, I insisted that the chairman draft a report detailing the seized question paper and provide an official receipt from a Vyapam officer to document our possession. He eventually complied with my request. When the sealed packets containing the question papers were opened the following day at the Subhash School examination centre in Bhopal, it was confirmed that Set A of the question paper matched the one seized by the police.

Upon receiving the report, the chairman cancelled the recruitment examination. The police launched a thorough investigation into the case, conducting raids at various locations across different states to uncover the truth. As a result of these raids, several individuals associated with the scam were apprehended.

The police spared no effort in attempting to uncover how the question papers were leaked but were unable to find any substantial leads. During the inquiry, the police visited a security printing press[*] in Gujarat where the papers were printed, but due to the leakproof system in place, obtaining the question papers from there proved impossible.

Attempts to trace the mobile numbers of certain Vyapam officials and place them on interception proved futile as their lack of cooperation hindered the investigation, preventing the

---

[*]A security printing press is a specialized facility that produces secure documents like banknotes, passports and identity cards. These presses use advanced printing technologies and security features to ensure authenticity and integrity by employing intricate designs, specialized inks and other measures to deter counterfeiting and protect sensitive information.

police from uncovering any clues about the main culprits. The case remained shrouded in mystery.

Leaks were also detected in the Patwari (revenue officials) examination. The police received a question paper faxed from a PCO on the night before the recruitment exams, but it was two years old. As no CCTV footage was available in the PCO, the police could not pursue any further investigation.

The Vyapam scam, centred around recruitment and professional exams, exposed a complex network of irregularities and organized criminal activities. It not only tarnished the image of Madhya Pradesh but also had far-reaching consequences. Despite efforts by law enforcement and inquiry agencies, corruption persisted due to Vyapam's failure to implement reforms. What began as isolated incidents in the mid-1990s escalated into a massive scandal when the first FIR was filed in Chhatarpur district in 2002.

The scammers adapted their methods to evade arrest and continued to profit. They advised candidates to leave their optical mark recognition (OMR) sheets blank, promising to fill in the marks themselves based on merit list requirements. The results were declared based on forged marks on the OMR sheets. Selected candidates later obtained their answer books through the Right to Information Act and filled in the blanks on the OMR sheets to match the marks already recorded for their selection. The amended OMR sheets were scanned again, and the records of the selected candidates were updated. This revealed flaws in regulatory mechanisms and the exploitation of legislation like the Right to Information Act.

Many involved, including Vyapam officers, were arrested, but corruption persisted. Candidates who had benefited faced arrest amidst false rumours of related suicides and murders. This exacerbated fear and scepticism. The scandal eroded public trust, both domestically and internationally. It serves as a cautionary tale, highlighting the need for systemic reforms and responsible governance. Only through collective effort can Madhya Pradesh restore its reputation and ensure fairness in future exams.

11

In the Veil of Darkness

A terrifying incident of a gang rape inside a moving car sent shockwaves through the very core of our community. The weight of this case rested heavily upon the shoulders of the police force, presenting us with a formidable challenge. The stage was set for an intense battle between justice and darkness, where every step we took in pursuit of the truth was filled with drama and uncertainty.

It was a clammy summer night, and only a few police officers were present at the Rajpur Road police station. Around 10.30 p.m., a man walked into the police station with a woman in torn clothes. He identified himself as Lallan Singh and the woman as his wife, Sapna, residents of Mumbai. Since Sapna's T-shirt was torn, the officers immediately gave her a T-shirt to cover herself.

He explained, 'I had gone to an ashram in the city with my wife, Sapna, in the morning for our daughter Ankita's admission into a school run by the ashram. After leaving the ashram we were standing on the road and waiting for a vehicle when a black Innova pulled up in front of us. The person sitting in the front told us to get inside and that he would drop us anywhere, so my wife and I got into it. The vehicle began moving towards Karaundi and then proceeded towards Rajpur Road.

'While the car was moving, three men who had been inside the car took turns to gang-rape my wife. One of them put a pistol against my forehead. I was so scared that I could not utter a single word. He then put the same pistol on my wife's chest as she was screaming a lot.'

Singh said that the criminals then dropped him and his wife 1 km from the Rajpur Road crossing in Bhopal. According to his judgement, the rapists seemed to be in their 40s. He then went on to describe the perpetrators: all three men were of medium height, dark-skinned, heavier than average people and clad in simple pants and shirts. Singh asserted that if they were brought in front of him, he would be able to identify them.

When the criminals dumped Singh and his wife, they also threw the carpet from the car, which had a used condom and a silver bracelet stuck to it. Lallan had brought these along; the silver bracelet had 'Tipoo' inscribed on it.

Preliminary interaction with the victims made it evident that the place from where they were picked up in the black Innova fell within the jurisdiction of the Nehru Sagar police station, so Lallan and Sapna were escorted in a police jeep to the Nehru Sagar police station by the Rajpur Road police.

The Nehru Sagar police immediately sent Sapna to Sultania Janana Hospital for a medical check-up. Because the police officers were busy at the hospital, they were unable to inform the senior officers about the incident. The local press, however, got information about the same from the hospital late at night.

❧

The next morning, newspaper headlines read: 'A woman gang-raped in a moving vehicle for several hours in the state capital. Victim says, "I was repeatedly gang raped. Although I kept screaming, no one heard anything. Nobody came to my rescue."'

Not only was the woman subjected to this heinous crime, but it also highlighted a breach in the law and order in the state's capital. Immediately after gathering the details of the incident from the police officers, I (then IG, Bhopal Zone) informed ADG (Intelligence) and the DGP about it. They directed me to speak to the chief minister. When I called him, he said he had already read about the incident in the newspaper and was disturbed by it. He lamented that the fear of the police seemed to have dissipated from the minds of criminals, sending a wrong message to residents that the administration had given free rein to wrongdoers. The chief minister also added that the police should act tough against the criminals, treat the common people gently and thoroughly probe the case to bring the culprits to justice. Failure to do so would result in grave consequences for the police force. I found no justifications or excuses to offer him, given the severity and implications of the crime. I discussed the issue with the DIG and SP over the phone, and both seemed very upset about it.

We proceeded to the Nehru Sagar police station to talk to the victim and her husband and gather more information about the incident, reaching the station around 10 a.m.

Lallan and Sapna had been sent to a hotel to rest and recuperate. We assumed that both must be trying to forget the trauma they had experienced. We instructed a female SI to bring them to the police station.

In the interim, we inspected the site where the victim and her husband had been dumped, along with the carpet and bracelet. Anurag Pandey, the in-charge of Nehru Sagar police station, had already examined the spot at night. We examined the spot with forensic experts but could not find any evidence. The location remained quite desolate during the daytime, and even fewer people were around at night. Therefore, there were barely any eyewitnesses. We spent two to three hours working at the crime scene before returning to the police station.

Though feeling a little tired, we never gave up hope of finding the culprits. We thought we could find some potential leads after discussing the issue with Sapna and Lallan. Our hopes were dashed when the female SI informed us that Sapna and Lallan had left the hotel without saying anything to anyone. We speculated that the traumatic incident might have forced them to leave the hotel. However, they did not inform anyone about their whereabouts and their mobile phones were also switched off.

In the meantime, I received a call from a person named Rajesh who identified himself as Sapna's brother-in-law. He informed us that he had complained to the National Commission for Women about the Bhopal police's lack of interest in the case. He claimed that Sapna was totally shattered and traumatized after the incident. I was surprised by his call because the incident had occurred only a few hours ago, and he had already sent a complaint to the National Commission for Women. Soon after, I received a call from my personal secretary, Jeetendra Thakur, informing me that the National Human Rights Commission had faxed me, asking for a detailed report of the incident, a copy of the FIR, the medical report of the victim and her statement, to be immediately faxed to the commission.

Thakur also said that the chief minister had received a volley of complaints about the incident from the Vidisha Krishi Upaj Mandi, Betul Krishi Upaj Mandi, various towns of Hoshangabad (now Narmadapuram) and many other areas of the state and that a report should be sent to the chief minister's office through the intelligence wing immediately.

Lallan and Sapna's sudden departure from the hotel raised suspicions but due to the sensitive nature of the crime, we refrained from discussing it. We tried to understand Sapna's perspective and how such trauma could influence behaviours or actions.

We were now looking for the next source of information and decided to go to the ashram. After going through the visitor's register at the ashram, the manager said he had no information about the couple's trip to the ashram. The manager's report deepened our suspicion about the incident. We formed two teams: one went to Balrampur, of which Sapna was a resident, to discuss the issue with the local police and find out some more details about the victim and her husband, while the other remained in Bhopal to mull over the case.

Our team in Bhopal came across a man called Tipoonath, who ran a food joint on Rajpur Road. His conduct raised suspicions. Tipoonath had a black-and-white Safari car and had been heavily intoxicated the night of the incident. Some officials believed that the couple might have misidentified Tipoonath's vehicle as the black Innova in their complaint. However, we couldn't verify the vehicle since Lallan and Sapna were unreachable.

When police arrived at Tipoonath's farmhouse, he was so tipsy that he was unable to speak. His black-and-white Safari had been recently cleaned, but there were footprints of a woman's sandals and mud stains on its roof. There were also some carpet threads like the one that Sapna and Lallan had brought to the police station. During the search of the farmhouse, a pistol-like weapon was found, but it was not in a working condition.

Based on the evidence, some officials said that the case had been worked out and that Tipoonath should immediately be taken into custody. They further said Tipoonath's accomplices could be arrested later. Nevertheless, after a discussion with the senior officers, I decided Tipoonath should be taken into custody for questioning only after he sobered up.

Meanwhile, Rajesh was repeatedly calling me to say how the incident had put his sister-in-law and brother in a bad state and to express concern over the police's inability to lay their hands on the rapists. He also sent fax messages to the police headquarters and chief minister's office. Rajesh was also using the National Human Rights Commission and the National Commission for Women to force us to arrest the culprits as early as possible. Pressure mounted as messages poured in from farmers of Vidisha, Hoshangabad and Betul to the chief minister's office. The newspapers tore into our efficiency, but we continued to work. We were unable to understand what invisible power was working against us.

In Balrampur, locals said that no woman named Sapna lived in the Gautam Buddha Nagar area. We were still searching in the dark. Subsequently, we decided to send a team led by SI Neeraj Verma to Mumbai since Lallan lived in Wadala, Mumbai.

We obtained public switched telephone network (PSTN) data

from all the towers in the areas the vehicle in which the woman was assaulted had passed. The cyber cell, led by SI Salil Sharma, was instructed to thoroughly study the PSTN data, focusing on mobile phones connected to towers along the vehicle's route. The numbers were high as those areas are bustling with activity throughout the day. We also gathered details of all black Innova cars registered in Madhya Pradesh from the Regional Transport Office and tried to match the owner's and driver's mobile numbers against the PSTN data. Unfortunately, our efforts yielded no leads and we remained in the dark.

Furthermore, we were also disturbed by the state government's warning that failure to arrest the culprits within 24 hours would result in disciplinary actions against some of the senior officers involved in the investigation. While transfers are routine in the police department, reassignment due to inefficiency is considered to be dishonourable. The Bhopal police was facing widespread criticism. Despite my officers' tireless efforts, we were still unable to trace the culprits, sparking outcry and severe condemnation from all corners. The SP also maintained excellent relations with the press and public; hence, I wondered what invisible power was defaming the Bhopal police and mounting pressure on the state government to act against us. On top of this, I was facing an unprecedented phenomenon—a rape victim vanishing after lodging a complaint.

In the meantime, Tipoonath had been brought in for questioning and confessed to the police that on the night of the incident, he had had consensual sex in a car with an unknown woman for which he had paid. Consequently, there was a suggestion to refrain from releasing Tipoonath and instead immediately arrest him, deferring the handling of his accomplices for later.

I still could not see any logic in taking Tipoonath into custody.

Hence, I turned down the proposal. A junior officer told a senior police officer at the headquarters that he had no other option but to arrest Tipoonath due to the glaring evidence against him. Tipoonath's whereabouts matched the time and location of the incident, and the engraving on the bracelet found also matched his. Moreover, his suspicious behaviour and admission of engaging in sexual activity with a woman in a vehicle at the time of the incident could not be overlooked, nor could the evidence collected from his vehicle be disregarded.

The superior officer from the police headquarters said to me, 'In trying to solve the case, if any officer wants to arrest Tipoonath, they are doing so at their own risk; you should not get in the way. If Tipoonath is innocent, the court will release him. The court should also get a chance to do its job.' I explained to my superior my belief that Tipoonath had not committed the crime. Despite his engagement in physical relations with a woman at the same time and place as the incident, it was consensual and transactional in nature.

I kept myself away from Tipoonath's arrest.

☙

Back in Balrampur, SI Deepak Khatri kept searching for Sapna. He also took the help of the Gautam Buddha Nagar police in Balrampur. Despite his efforts, he returned disappointed, unable to locate her anywhere in Balrampur. When he reported his lack of progress to me over the phone, I reiterated my instruction: 'Come what may, you have to find her.'

On receiving my instructions, Khatri was so upset that he slumped down on the floor of the police station. When a sentry posted at the police station saw Khatri sitting in that manner, he asked him what the matter was. Khatri explained his mission to find a woman named Sapna but had been unable to locate her anywhere.

Khatri said, 'If I return to Bhopal empty-handed, the IG will suspend me.' Frustrated by his inability to locate Sapna, Khatri resorted to using an inappropriate term out of his exasperation while talking to the sentry. As soon as the sentry heard Sapna's name, he told Khatri that there was a sex worker by that name in the red-light area of Kandhar Bagh. The sentry continued, 'I will take you to Sapna.'

At this, a smile flashed on Khatri's face. He seemed to have gotten a new lease of life. They immediately left for the red-light area with some other officers. By the time Khatri reached the area, dusk was falling.

When the police team arrived at Sapna's doorstep, they saw her preparing for customers. Sapna and Khatri looked at each other.

Just as Khatri said, 'Sapna?' she replied, 'From Bhopal?'

Khatri asked Sapna to come along with him. It was not easy to take her out of the red-light area because all the women of that place surrounded the police team, saying they would not let Khatri take Sapna to Bhopal. The police station guard who had accompanied Khatri called other cops to the spot. They decided to bring Sapna first to the Gautam Buddha Nagar police station, and the women finally dispersed.

Excitedly, Khatri informed the SP in Bhopal and other officers about it over the phone. The SP directed Khatri to leave for Bhopal with Sapna. After a while, Khatri called the SP again, saying, 'The local police officers are not allowing me to bring Sapna to Bhopal. Please talk to the senior officers.'

The SP spoke to me and requested I talk to the IG of Balrampur range so that Sapna could be brought to Bhopal.

When I spoke to my counterpart in Balrampur, he said, 'I

will allow you to take Sapna to Bhopal only if a woman police officer accompanies her.'

Recognizing the protocol, I immediately sent ASP Ruchi Vardhan, City SP Dilip Singh Tomar and a few other officers to Balrampur by road. The team reached Balrampur at noon the next day. They completed all the formalities and brought Sapna to Bhopal the following morning.

On their way back, Ruchi informed me over the phone, 'Sapna is unmarried. Lallan is not her husband, but she has not revealed any information about the crime. Anyway, when she gets comfortable with us, she will disclose everything. At the moment, the gang-rape incident seems suspicious.'

The revelation that Sapna was not Lallan's wife slowly started lifting the veil of mystery surrounding the case. It was clear that someone had cooked up the gang-rape story. Rajesh, who had repeatedly been calling us earlier, suddenly disappeared from the scene and switched off his phone. Our attempts to trace him through call details proved futile because we realized he was using some fictitious identity and number.

Though finally locating Sapna brought some relief, it also left us with some questions: What prompted someone to file a false complaint? Who were the individuals behind it? And why did they choose Bhopal to lodge such an accusation, where the chief minister was so sensitive about crimes against women that he personally monitored the progress of such cases until the wrongdoer was tried and convicted?

The next day, after Sapna arrived from Balrampur with the police team, the SP called me at 11 a.m. and asked, 'Should we go to Nehru Sagar police station so that we may talk to the woman and extract information from her?' I informed the DGP about the investigation's progress, who later visited the police station and spoke to Sapna.

The SP and I reached the Nehru Sagar police station with the DIG of Bhopal. All of us congratulated Ruchi, Dilip and Khatri for their efforts. I personally commended Khatri on his achievement, embracing and encouraging him to continue doing such good work in the future.

After Sapna had breakfast, Ruchi and I began to speak to her. We told her to tell us without fear what had happened. Sapna said that she lived in the red-light area of Balrampur but was not married to Lallan. 'Although I'm unmarried, I had an affair with a man named Mahesh Singh and we had a daughter named Ankita. Mahesh is no more,' she informed us.

She revealed that she had been a performer in a pub in Mumbai when she first met Lallan. Sapna said that Lallan had told her to accompany him to Bhopal, promising to pay her ₹20,000 if she accepted. Lallan took her from Mumbai to Surat, from where they came to Bhopal by the Ahmedabad–Bhopal Express on the day of the incident. She and Lallan then loitered around Bhopal the whole day before going to the ashram. As Sapna continued her story, her voice faltered and tears trickled down her cheeks.

Sapna said that in Bhopal, she had visited the ashram during the day to get information about the admission process in their school. The management of the ashram said that as Ankita was only three and a half years old, she could not be admitted. She also revealed that Lallan had intentionally not written their name and address in the ashram's register. That was why the ashram management could not tell the police about their visit.

'When we came out of the ashram, it was 8.30 p.m. We were waiting for a vehicle on the road, and a luxury car stopped near us. It was Rajesh and Sanjay, whom we had met earlier in Surat. Lallan told me to get inside the car, and I did whatever he asked me to do.

'Sanjay and Lallan were sitting on my left and right sides, respectively. As the vehicle lurched forward, Rajesh told the driver to stop it and sit with all of us in the back seat. All three of them then began to molest me and instructed me not to yell. They tore my clothes and raped me for more than an hour. After raping me, Sanjay and Rajesh dropped Lallan and me on Rajpur Road, threatening to wipe out my family if I ever tried to disclose the incident to anyone,' Sapna revealed.

She further told us that Lallan said he would be filing a complaint with the police and that she should not disclose the names of those who had violated her. Instead, she should inform the police that some unknown people had raped her.

Sapna said that Lallan had taken her to the police station. She was so scared that she was barely able to say anything. She said she was doing exactly what Lallan had wanted her to. Because she feared him, she had not mentioned the rapists' names back then.

When they disappeared from the hotel, Lallan had taken her to Surat, where Sanjay and Rajesh spoke to her again. Lallan then took her to Mumbai before ultimately bringing her back to Balrampur.

❧

Our team in Mumbai discovered that Lallan was not at his house. They came to know through his neighbours that Lallan was originally from Bihar, unmarried and worked as a bartender at a pub. When the police inquired about him at the pub, the workers said that he had quit the job a few months ago and gone back to Bihar. They further revealed that he had been in contact with a few people from Surat who used to visit him. Lallan spoke to them in hush-hush tones and used to see them off at the pub's gate. He had visited Surat twice or thrice in the past three to four months. The police team collected Lallan's residential address in Bihar and left for that place.

They reached Lallan's house in Bihar two days later and brought him to Bhopal. When Lallan was questioned, he confirmed that he got acquainted with Sapna at an orchestra party and became friends with her. Lallan was introduced to Rajesh and Sanjay at one of these parties.

Lallan said that both had asked him to find a beautiful, smart and compliant girl. Lallan said, 'The duo had given me ₹1 lakh and told me to reach Surat with the girl, after which they would tell me what to do. I saw Sapna performing at a bar and told her that I had some work for which she would get a good amount of money.'

Lallan continued, 'Sapna wanted to know about the work, but I told her that we had to go to Surat where we would be informed about it. We reached Surat and met Rajesh at a hotel. We were asked to go to Bhopal where we would be informed about the next steps.'

Lallan said that he and Sapna then returned to Mumbai. After a few days, Rajesh called Lallan and Sapna to Surat again. Rajesh told them to reach Bhopal by the evening train that would arrive there in the morning. Rajesh and Sanjay would be there. Rajesh gave two tickets to Lallan, using which he and Sapna arrived at Habibganj railway station in the morning. Rajesh met them at the railway station and gave Lallan some money for food and lodging before dropping them near the ashram, where they stayed and had lunch. They then went to the ashram, where they were denied admission for Sapna's daughter, and then encountered Rajesh and Sanjay in their car.

'They said that they would drop us near a police station where we had to lodge a complaint that three unidentified criminals had raped Sapna in a moving car at gunpoint for one hour. I was told to say that as the crime was committed at gunpoint, I could not fight back and that the crooks tore Sapna's shirt. They also told me that they had thrown out the bracelet and the carpet.

'Then they handed a filled condom to me, which they had obtained through their driver to prove that Sapna was raped. Both Rajesh and Sanjay raped Sapna and also forced me to have physical relations with her to corroborate the rape story.

'They showed us the police station from the road and dropped us near the highway, from where we walked up to the Rajpur Road police station, from where they took us to the Nehru Sagar police station.

'There, I lodged a complaint on the grounds of what Rajesh had told us and handed over the broken bracelet, torn carpet and used condom to the police as evidence. Once Sapna's medical examination was complete, the police took us to a hotel and said that they would talk to us in the morning. However, we set out for Mumbai via Surat early in the morning. On reaching Mumbai, I bought a few articles for Sapna, dropped her at Balrampur and left for Patna,' said Lallan.

He further said that he had no knowledge of Rajesh's or Sanjay's whereabouts or of the identity of the driver. He also did not know anything about the purpose behind the whole plan. When the police asked him about the person named 'Tipoo', Lallan pleaded ignorance.

❦

While Lallan was being interrogated, Tipoonath was sitting in another room at the police station. As soon as the police brought

Tipoonath in front of Lallan, he almost jumped from his chair and said that it was Tipoonath who had been the third person in the car. Given the delicate situation, we did not bring Tipoonath and Sapna face to face but she did corroborate whatever Lallan had disclosed about Rajesh and Sanjay.

Releasing Tipoonath became challenging for the police due to his mobile tower location in various areas the car had passed through. Additionally, evidence such as a fragment of a broken bracelet, a thread from the torn carpet found in his car and his identification by Lallan added to the complexity of the situation. He was taken into custody as there was strong evidence against him. The police had to call Sapna back from Balrampur to identify Tipoonath in judicial custody in front of an executive magistrate. Due to inconsistencies in their statements, she was presented before the executive magistrate in the absence of police to ensure she spoke truthfully without any fear as per legal protocol. She denied that Tipoonath had any links with the incident.

❧

In the meantime, IPS Gautam Sawang, a batchmate of mine, came to Bhopal and stayed in Hotel Palace.

When I went to the hotel to have dinner with my friend, I called the manager and asked about those who were lodged there around the date of the incident. When I inspected the hotel's occupancy register, I came across the name of Dr Bharti. The manager said that the conduct of that person had been highly suspicious. He had arrived with a girl on the morning flight, but the girl left him in the hotel and went away. He was to leave the hotel the next morning, but he created a lot of fuss at night and returned to Surat by taxi that night itself.

We found his mobile number in the hotel register. When I

spoke to him over the phone, he informed me about what had happened and about two folks named Rani Das and Ajay Mohan.

According to Dr Bharti, Rani Das had brought him to Bhopal on a Jet Airways morning flight, and that he had seen Rani Das conversing with two people seated near the back of the plane. Based on the seat numbers indicated by Dr Bharti, we extracted the records from the Jet Airways' office and came to know that those persons were Tipoonarayan and Ramesh Gilani.

The next day, the police traced their records in various hotels and discovered that the duo had been in Hotel Lake View, Samrat. Their mobile numbers were also recovered from the hotel records. Further, records of Rani Das were found in Hotel Lake View, Sudarshan. Ajay Mohan, who had booked the hotel rooms, also stayed at Hotel Lake View, Sudarshan.

With the appearance of these characters, the case seemed to be turning more and more complicated.

Subsequent investigations revealed that Rajesh and Sanjay were aliases and their real names were Kanha Ramani and Radhey Ramani, respectively. The Ramani brothers, originally from Jhabua, Madhya Pradesh, had planned the gang-rape to take revenge against their rivals.

Kanha Ramani had a business tie-up with a person named Asnani and had invested ₹600 crore in his firm. After becoming a partner in Asnani's firm, Kanha managed to secure a loan of ₹2,000 crore from a bank for the business's promotion and took control of Asnani's business through fraudulent means. Consequently, Asnani had been after Kanha's blood since then.

Asnani gave ₹50 lakh to a senior officer and got Kanha arrested in a fake case under the Narcotics Act in Gujarat. Not to be outdone, Kanha retaliated by framing Asnani in a similar case under the Narcotics Act in Madhya Pradesh.

When Kanha was in jail, he befriended the jail physician, Dr Bharti, who got him released on bail through a fake medical certificate. However, the Supreme Court intervened when Asnani raised concerns about the authenticity of Kanha's medical certificate. The apex court sought a proper medical certificate from a reputed doctor. Kanha tried to get a fake certificate from the owner of the Shankar Cardiac Institute, Dr Sudarshan Shankar, but he refused to give it. The Supreme Court cancelled Kanha Ramani's bail application, but he managed to run away.

Dr Bharti had taken ₹2 crore from Kanha Ramani for providing him with special facilities inside the prison and arranging a fake medical certificate. Because Dr Bharti failed to deliver on his promises, the Ramanis wanted to teach him a lesson.

The Ramanis had set up a bogus firm called GST with Ramesh Gilani and Tipoonarayan in Surat, Gujarat. They gave a bribe of ₹25 lakh to a bank manager and obtained a loan of ₹2,500 crore. After withdrawing the first instalment of ₹1,200 crore, all four (the Ramani brothers, Gilani and Tipoonarayan) became defaulters.

The strained relationship between the Ramani brothers and their associates led to the concoction of a plan to implicate Dr Bharti, Dr Shankar, Gilani and Tipoonarayan in a gang-rape case as a means of revenge.

❧

The Ramanis were aware that because Dr Bharti, Dr Shankar, Tipoonarayan and Gilani were renowned people and had political backing in Gujarat, they could not be trapped in that state. So they decided to call them to Bhopal, where the Ramanis had mustered the support of some influential person.

Kanha set up two teams to get their plan in motion. One team consisted of Lallan and Sapna, and the other of Ajay Mohan from Mumbai and Rani Das, a resident of Khandwa and a student at a premier management institute. Rani Das and Ajay Mohan were told that they would get ₹20 lakh after the job was completed.

Kanha Ramani once mentioned to Rani Das and Ajay Mohan that nobody could be saved if an FIR was registered in two cases: one for bouncing a cheque and the other for violating a woman.

To add legitimacy to their scheme, the Ramanis set up a fake office through Rani Das and Ajay Mohan in Ahmedabad, and they were asked to prepare a fake project report for opening a medical college worth ₹2,000 crore in Bhopal.

First, Rani Das gained Dr Bharti's trust by engaging in physical relations with him and manipulating him. With the help of Dr Bharti, Ajay and Rani met Dr Shankar and informed him about the project in Bhopal. Dr Shankar was also told that he would be appointed as the director of the proposed medical college. Dr Shankar then told them to bring the full report to him.

Then, Rani and Ajay brought Ramesh Gilani and Tipoonarayan on to the scene. When they agreed to the project, they were told to reach Bhopal on a fixed date. They told Dr Bharti, Tipoonarayan, Gilani and Dr Shankar that a former chief minister of Madhya Pradesh was a partner in the project and had prepared the blueprint. Dr Shankar was also told that initially ₹2,000 crore would be spent on the medical college and an additional amount of ₹4,000 crore would be invested afterwards.

Rani and Ajay went to Dr Shankar with the project report and told him to go to Bhopal on the due date. He agreed to go there. However, upon reviewing the project report, Dr Shankar found it unviable and decided against going to Bhopal. He, however, said nothing to Ajay or Rani about it. Ajay booked air tickets for four and told Rani to take Dr Bharti to Bhopal by a Jet Airways flight in the morning. They were told that a meeting would be held with the former chief minister.

Ajay also said to Tipoonarayan, 'Whenever a meeting with an important person takes place, the VVIP gives a present to that person as a souvenir.'

Ajay instructed Tipoonarayan to buy a silver bracelet with his nickname engraved on it and send it through courier to Ajay Mohan's address in Mumbai. He would hand it over to the former chief minister who, in turn, would give it to Tipoonarayan as a gift at the meeting. Therefore, Tipoonarayan's name was engraved on it as 'Tipoo'.

Tipoonarayan, Gilani and Dr Bharti arrived at Bhopal airport, and Ajay and Rani took them to different hotels in the city.

The conspirators decided that Rani Das would be with Dr Bharti in one car and Ajay Mohan would be with Tipoonarayan and Ramesh Gilani in another. On the pretext of introducing the trio to the former chief minister, they would move around the airport for an hour to establish their physical presence in the area; after a while, they would be informed that the former chief minister had some other engagement, so he would not be able to meet them then and would meet later.

During the day, one of them slept with Rani Das, who handed over the used condoms to Kanha Ramani. In the evening, when they were told that the meeting with the former chief minister was cancelled, Dr Bharti returned to his hotel room. Just as he switched on the TV, he found the former chief minister addressing a function in New Delhi. He realized there had been some conspiracy and returned to Surat by road. Gilani and Tipoonarayan also felt that something was wrong. They also left for Surat the next day.

Ajay Mohan and Rani Das set out for Mumbai. They had no idea about the alleged gang rape.

❧

The Ramanis intended to incriminate their targets using fabricated evidence, such as the used condom and bracelet provided by Rani Das. They believed that forensic analysis would implicate Gilani, Tipoonarayan and Dr Bharti, resulting in their imprisonment. However, their plan ultimately failed, and an innocent man, Tipoonath, was wrongfully accused and detained. Tipoonath was ultimately released based on Sapna's statement and the fact that the broken part of the bracelet found in his vehicle did not match the one bought as a present for the former chief minister.

The investigation into the case was an arduous process, marked by sleepless nights and intense scrutiny. Unfortunately, later, a weight of disappointment settled heavily on our shoulders as we listened to the judge's verdict. The accused were set free, their faces masked with smug satisfaction. Despite our relentless pursuit of justice, the outcome slipped through our fingers like sand. We had painstakingly unravelled the threads of this crime and pieced together all the evidence to build a compelling case. However, the turning tides of witness testimonies and shortcomings in our presentation had robbed us of the victory we had so desperately sought.

As we heard the judicial verdict that day with heads held high but hearts heavy, we knew that the truth we had uncovered would forever remain buried beneath legal intricacies. Though justice may have been elusive at that moment, we were determined to persevere. The truth we uncovered would not be forgotten, and we pledged to continue our fight against those who preyed on the innocent. In the face of adversity, our dedication remained unwavering, keeping the hope of justice alive.

Then There Was a Bus Ticket

For over three decades, the notorious outlaw Hathi Raja unleashed a reign of terror in Bundelkhand, leaving a trail of bloodshed and violated souls in his wake. One fateful day, the intricate threads of justice began to tighten around him, ensnaring the felon within the grasp of law enforcement.

During my time as IG of Bhopal, the municipal corporation elections were under way. I was strolling through the old areas of the city with the commissioner of Bhopal when I received a message on my wireless set informing me that a young girl's body had been found in a sack near the Chaurai crossing in Rajpur area, which falls under the Baloda police station. The area was located near the railway lines.

Within a few seconds, another message came over the wireless that the DIG of Bhopal, with his team, was observing the elections in Baloda. I immediately spoke to DIG Ashok Awasthi over the phone and asked him to go to the spot and provide me with details of the incident.

Awasthi examined the body with the help of some female officers. The SDO of police, who oversaw the Baloda police station, and other staff were also present at the site.

Apart from the body, there was barely any evidence at the site. However, a few yards from the spot, some marks of a jeep's tyres were found. These marks suggested that the body had been placed inside a sack elsewhere and then transported to this area for disposal.

The boundary of the Mandideep police station in Raisen district was just 100 m from where the body was found. Those who threw the body were perhaps in a hurry and had no knowledge about the boundaries of different police stations. Hence, they discarded it in an area falling under the Baloda police station's jurisdiction. Had the body been found on the railway tracks, the case would have fallen under the jurisdiction of the Raisen district police. This could have given the murderers a time advantage, as it would have taken senior police officers some time to reach the remote location.

We interacted with the residents of the area, but they failed to provide any clue about the culprits.

The police assumed that the body had been discarded early in the morning near the railway station. The criminals, fearing that someone might see them, had disposed of the body near the railway lines instead of casting it off on to the tracks. Had the body been removed from the sack and placed on the railway tracks, the killers could have easily passed off the murder as a suicide.

The female officers examined the body and inferred that the murdered woman was around 24 years old. There was no further evidence to identify the body. Awasthi instructed them to check the woman's jeans, but the body had swollen so much that the jeans got stuck to it.

After some effort, the female cops retrieved a Volvo bus ticket from the back pocket of the jeans. The ticket indicated travel from Indore to Bhopal. A mobile phone number was found written on the back of the ticket.

The police sent the body for a post-mortem examination, and the staff left for Baloda police station along with Awasthi. In the meantime, the SP of Bhopal, Jaydeep Prasad, also reached the police station. They provided me with detailed information about the incident. Additionally, with the ongoing elections in Bhopal, most of the senior officers were on the move. As news about the incident spread, all the senior officers promptly reached the site.

⚬﹏⚬

The police rang the number found on the back of the bus ticket, and a girl named Kavita picked up. She said that she had left Bhopal for Aligarh by the Shatabdi Express the previous evening. She and her friend Radhika had come to Bhopal from Indore on a Volvo bus. We presumed that the murdered girl was most likely Radhika based on the ticket we had found.

While the murderers had not left behind any evidence, the

body's swelling after the death had prevented them from retrieving the bus ticket from Radhika's jeans pocket. Without the ticket, the cops would not have been able to identify the body so quickly. Kavita and Radhika were students at the National School of Design and residents of Harpalpur. Another girl named Nikita had also accompanied Kavita and Radhika to Indore and then returned to Bhopal. All three girls used to live in a hostel in Bhopal.

Kavita informed the police that Radhika's granduncle lived in Vasundhara Vihar Colony in Kamla Nagar, Bhopal. She mentioned that Radhika had been picked up by her granduncle's car from the bus stop upon their return from Indore. With this information, we sent a team to Vasundhara Vihar Colony.

Upon arrival at Radhika's granduncle's house in Vasundhara Vihar Colony, the team found the premises deserted, with the door of the house bolted from the outside. The officers broke open the door and went inside. The house was in a mess—the gas was on, the kitchen tap was running, rooms were flooded and utensils were scattered everywhere. It seemed as if someone had fled in a hurry.

Neighbours gathered outside the house upon seeing the police officers. They said that the house belonged to Rajendra Singh Bhatia, also known as Hathi Raja. They also said Hathi Raja had been present in the house with some people the previous night, including his son. However, they left the house early in the morning without saying anything to anyone in the area.

The team reported to me their discovery. Hailing from Bundelkhand, I recognized the significance of the name, as I had heard numerous stories about Hathi Raja. He was not only a notorious criminal but had also become a member of the legislative assembly (MLA) of Madhya Pradesh. He wielded significant influence over Harpalpur and the entire Bundelkhand region.

Hathi Raja had allegedly killed more than 100 people, but their bodies had never been discovered. Rumours suggested that he had constructed a pond in his house where he kept crocodiles and that he threw the bodies into it for the crocodiles to feast on. Cases had been registered against him in multiple police stations across Harpalpur, Khanna, Tikamgarh, Bhind, Morena, Jhansi and Sagar. Hathi Raja started his political career as a student leader and had served two terms as a legislator from Khanna district, contesting in the assembly elections from Kumaun Jail. He held the post of chairman of the Khanna District Cooperative Bank for 20 years and was associated with many political parties, for whom he handled many important assignments.

Hathi Raja had been jailed for killing a relative of the then Union home minister. His terror in the area was evident from the slogan that had been written when he was contesting the assembly election: 'Mohar lagegi haathi par nahin to goli lagegi chhati par' (Either vote for the elephant symbol or be ready to face bullets). This slogan was prominently displayed at various locations.

Hathi Raja's first wife, Mallika, was also actively involved in politics. Initially, she served as the chairperson of the district panchayat and later won the assembly election on a ticket from the then ruling party. Although Mallika was a legislator of the ruling party, the chief minister did not intervene in police actions against her husband. Instead, he allowed the law enforcement authorities a free hand to combat crimes perpetrated by Hathi Raja and his associates, particularly those targeting women.

❧

Our subsequent investigations revealed that Mrityunjay Singh, Hathi Raja's nephew, was Radhika's father. Thus, Radhika was the grandniece of the notorious gangster.

In the meantime, I spoke to the doctor who had conducted Radhika's post-mortem. What he said could send a shiver down anybody's spine. The doctor said that the girl was subjected to inhuman torture throughout the night before ultimately being shot with a .315 bore country-made gun. The bullet hit her in the head and she died. Upon hearing this, we sent a team to Harpalpur to gather a first-hand account of the relationship between Hathi Raja and his nephew Mrityunjay Singh.

The news of the murder spread like wildfire. As I was devising a strategy to work out the case in the crime branch office, the SDO of police from Ujjain Range entered my chamber. He identified himself as Radhika's maternal uncle and expressed his desire to claim her body.

I said, 'You are a senior police officer. You have left your place of work and come to Bhopal. Did you take permission from your seniors before doing that?'

He had no answer. He only reiterated that he had come to Bhopal to take Radhika's body to Harpalpur for the last rites. We did not let him take the body, insisting that it would be handed over only to her parents. The SDO informed Hathi Raja about our decision not to hand over the body to him. Hathi Raja resorted to calling and threatening my family members and friends, saying that the police should hand over the body of his granddaughter for cremation, claiming that tension would persist in Harpalpur until her last rites were performed. I told my acquaintances that the issue was very sensitive and that the law of the land should be allowed to take its course.

Because I stuck to my guns, Hathi Raja began using his political clout. A former chief minister, with whom I had worked and held in high esteem, contacted me after Hathi Raja sought clarification on why Radhika's body had not been handed over to the SDO. I informed the former chief minister about Hathi

Raja's background and the circumstances surrounding the murder. He had already been aware of Hathi Raja's criminal activities. I assured him that Radhika's body would only be handed over to her parents. He advised me to continue with the probe and instructed that if her parents contacted me directly, I should comply with their wishes.

Shortly afterwards, I got a call from a woman claiming to be Arati Singh, Radhika's mother. She explained that Radhika's father had recently suffered a leg injury in an accident and was unable to travel. She requested that the body be handed over to the police officer. I was wary of what the woman had said. I requested her to come to Bhopal to take the body. Before I could finish speaking, she burst into tears and abruptly ended the call.

Meanwhile, my team had reached Harpalpur. They reported that Mallika and her supporters had gathered at Mrityunjay Singh's house. The news of Radhika's murder had left her parents devastated and they were in shock.

I instructed the police team to bring Hathi Raja's driver, who had been present at the Vasundhara Vihar Colony residence on the night of the incident, to Bhopal for questioning. I also told them to speak to Mrityunjay Singh, and if he was unable to travel, he should send his wife with the police force to Bhopal. After a while, the team members informed me that they would reach Bhopal along with Hathi Raja's driver Hariram and Arati Singh.

The next day, our team arrived in Bhopal with Arati Singh and Hariram. I sent Hariram to the Baloda police station while I went to the crime branch to meet Arati Singh and offered my condolences for her daughter's untimely death. We offered her tea and breakfast. During our conversation, I told Arati that the government was very concerned about the incident and expressed my commitment to ensuring that the perpetrator would be brought to justice. In response, Arati broke into tears and began to recount the troubling relationship between her family and Hathi Raja. She revealed that sensing some malicious intent towards their daughter from Hathi Raja, her husband had performed a symbolic act of subservience by washing Hathi Raja's feet and drinking the water. This act, she explained, was done out of fear and coercion, as her husband sought to protect their family from the malevolent intentions of the notorious criminal.

Arati recounted her family's efforts to shield their daughter from Hathi Raja's influence, including sending her away to Jabalpur and later enrolling her in the National School of Design in Bhopal. Despite their precautions, Radhika still fell into Hathi Raja's trap upon returning from Indore. Arati said that she did not realize that the rogue would continue pursuing her daughter. Radhika had visited Harpalpur five days before her murder and showed Hathi Raja's photograph, saying that he had done something wrong to her but she could not tell anyone about it. Arati also revealed that recently a sessions court had acquitted Hathi Raja of a murder charge due to her husband Mrityunjay's legal intervention.

When I asked her the reasons for not coming to Bhopal to claim Radhika's body and instead asking me to hand it over to the SDO, Arati denied making any such call. She speculated that it might have been another woman acting on Hathi Raja's instructions.

Arati said that she had wanted to meet me but Mallika had come to her house along with her followers and had started performing some rituals. Hence, she hadn't been able to leave her house. She appreciated the police department's decision to bring her to Bhopal to collect the body.

Arati also suggested interrogating Hathi Raja's driver: 'Hathi Raja trusts his driver Hariram. He has a lot of information, and if you strictly interrogate him, he will blurt out everything he knows about the goon.'

She requested to see the spot where her daughter had been found, so I arranged for her to visit the site with a police team. We then escorted her back to Harpalpur with Radhika's body.

By the time Arati left for Harpalpur, we had a strong suspicion about who had committed the crime. The police took Hariram into custody, and under rigorous questioning, he confessed to his involvement. Hariram confessed to driving Hathi Raja's car and disposing of Radhika's body in the Baloda area. According to his testimony, the initial plan was to stage Radhika's death as a suicide by placing her body on the railway tracks. However, he had to abandon that plan as he had spotted a police jeep a few metres from the tracks. In a hurry, he was unable to remove the body from the sack, so he simply threw it a few yards away from the railway tracks and escaped.

Hariram revealed that Radhika had been shot dead in Hathi Raja's house at Vasundhara Vihar Colony. They had been aware of the Baloda area's jurisdiction belonging to Mandideep and the alertness of the police in Bhopal, which led them to prefer disposing of the body elsewhere. However, circumstances forced them to leave the body in the state capital.

We sifted through all the evidence step by step. Our team conducted thorough examinations of Hathi Raja's Vasundhara Vihar Colony house many times, as well as the site where Radhika's body was found. We also interviewed Radhika's friends at the National School of Design and summoned Kavita from

Aligarh to Bhopal. Our aim was to smoke out all the evidence.

✌

On the day of Radhika's last rites, Hathi Raja turned up at the spot where the rites were being performed. When journalists questioned him about the evidence related to the murder, he challenged them to present any proof they had. He brazenly claimed that although he had been accused in a hundred murder cases, there was no evidence to support the allegations, and thus, the police could never arrest him.

After the last rites were over, Mrityunjay Singh came to Bhopal. He expressed his disdain for Hathi Raja, describing him as the most despicable villain he had ever encountered.

'Hathi Raja had a strained relationship with the MP from Harpalpur. Concerned that the MP was trying to turn us against him and his wife, Hathi Raja cautioned me not to be swayed by the MP's influence. However, the MP displayed minimal interest in Hathi Raja's affairs.'

In the meantime, Hathi Raja himself arrived in Bhopal and stayed in the rest house meant for legislators. He did that just to show the police how influential he was.

Amidst these developments, the SP was transferred, and DIG Bhopal Ashok Awasthi assumed all responsibilities. Hathi Raja, aware of Awasthi's prior investigation against him, harboured a deep fear of the DIG.

Realizing that his political clout and muscle power would hardly have any impact on the Bhopal police, Hathi Raja tried to meet the chief minister, leveraging his wife's position as a lawmaker. However, his efforts were in vain. He then resorted to launching a misinformation campaign against Awasthi through TV channels. When that also failed, he got himself admitted to a private hospital on the pretext of an illness.

Immediately after that I contacted the chief minister. Despite Hathi Raja's wife holding a legislative assembly seat, the chief minister prioritized public welfare over political affiliations and urged me to act without fear.

I sent Bhupendra Singh, the TI of Baloda police station, to the private hospital where Hathi Raja was admitted on the pretext of illness to evade arrest. Confronting the doctor, I admonished him for admitting the criminal without valid cause, warning of repercussions. Fearing the consequences, the doctor promptly discharged Hathi Raja.

As soon as he was out of the hospital, we arrested him and brought him to the Baloda police station. This led to Mallika staging a protest with her supporters outside the DGP's residence.

Some of my senior colleagues believed the arrest was premature and would incur backlash from the government; I did not agree with them. I knew that the inquiry we were conducting was based on solid evidence. We handcuffed Hathi Raja, took him to Harpalpur at night and recovered the firearm that was used to kill Radhika. The residents of Harpalpur witnessed the perpetrator for the first time in such a deplorable state. Despite having eliminated evidence in the past after murdering over a hundred individuals, his role in his granddaughter's death would not go unpunished. With the firearm in hand, our team returned to Bhopal.

Besides his driver, Hathi Raja's nephew was also involved in the murder. Subsequently, the police caught the nephew and sent him to jail.

‿✶‿

As we began to sift through Hathi Raja's files, we came across his maid Neetu Singh's suicide. A case of unnatural death had been registered at Ramnagar police station. A few people had been probed in connection with the case, but it was closed after the post-mortem of the body.

Reopening the file related to Neetu Singh's suicide, we came to know that she had been the sarpanch (head) of a village in Khanna district. I assigned the task of reinvestigating the mysterious death to ASP Awadh Kishore Pandey, who dove right into it. Pandey learnt that Neetu Singh had immolated herself under mysterious circumstances by dousing her body with kerosene on the roof of a house in Vasundhara Vihar Colony.

Her body had been sent to Hamidia Hospital in Bhopal for post-mortem. Hathi Raja's wife, Mallika, who had been the chairperson of the district panchayat at that time, declared in writing that Neetu had no next of kin, so her body should be handed over to Mallika. Mallika claimed the body and asked Hathi Raja's driver Hariram to perform the last rites.

A police team led by Pandey visited Khanna district, where they came to know about Hathi Raja's predatory pursuit of Neetu Singh. The goon had coerced her into domestic servitude after separating her from her mentally disabled husband and son. With Mallika's support, Hathi Raja subjected Neetu Singh to repeated sexual harassment.

Driven to despair, Neetu Singh tragically ended her life by setting herself on fire at the house where Hathi Raja resided. Subsequently, Pandey instructed the authorities at Ramnagar police station to initiate a case against Hathi Raja and Mallika for their role in forcing Neetu Singh to commit suicide.

However, some of my senior colleagues disagreed with registering a case against Mallika. They said that on grounds of weak evidence, a legislator cannot be accused in such a sensitive case and that more thought should have been given before acting in a hurry.

As soon as a case was registered against Mallika, she escaped to Nepal. During the inquiry, the police searched for Neetu Singh's husband and son in Delhi and brought them to Bhopal to record their statements.

We had enough evidence, so we completed the investigation and filed a chargesheet in the court. The sessions court declared Mallika an absconder and issued her arrest warrant. By then, Mallika had returned from Nepal and was living in a minister's farmhouse. I informed the chief minister and home minister about the situation and requested them to advise the minister accordingly to prevent potential embarrassment for the government should the matter leak to the media.

Apart from the pressure of arrest, her membership in the assembly was also on the verge of being cancelled as she had been absconding for more than a year—Mallika had no choice but to surrender. For that reason, she reached a court in Bhopal to surrender. The case diary had not reached the court by that time and the police were asked to present it. Fearing arrest, Mallika sought refuge inside the assembly. Nonetheless, as soon as the police came to know of it, they encircled the assembly building.

I informed the chief minister and speaker of the assembly about her presence. I told them that the police had an arrest warrant against her and wanted to arrest her for her role in her maid's suicide. The chief minister and speaker were aware of the case. They said that the House would function till the evening and instead of arresting her from the assembly, the police should wait until she left the building.

When Mallika emerged from the assembly in the evening, the police arrested her. Despite her insistence on using her own vehicle, she was escorted to the court in a police vehicle. After a prolonged trial, the sessions court sentenced both Hathi Raja and Mallika to 10 years in jail for Neetu Singh's suicide case.

❦

In the meantime, Hathi Raja and his accomplices, who were involved in Radhika's murder, were sentenced to life imprisonment.

Hathi Raja moved from the high court to the Supreme Court for bail. Everyone, including Radhika's father, who had contested several cases on behalf of the goon, had already anticipated this move. Aware of Hathi Raja's tactics and determined to seek justice for his deceased daughter, Radhika's father spared no effort to ensure the goon remained behind bars. Everybody also knew that once Hathi Raja was out of jail, he would manipulate evidence and it would be difficult to punish him and his wife under the law.

Eventually, justice took its course and Hathi Raja was sent to jail. However, he pretended to be ill to secure a transfer to the All India Institute of Medical Sciences (AIIMS), Delhi, for treatment, citing that he was not getting proper medical attention in Bhopal Jail. The high court stated that a medical board should be set up to examine Hathi Raja, and only after that he would be allowed to be admitted to AIIMS or given bail. Hathi Raja knew that if he faced the medical board, his plan would be exposed because he was not actually ill. He tried to appoint doctors who would work for him, but because of the measures taken by the police, he failed to do that.

In a twist of fate, Hathi Raja's elaborate ruse to deceive the medical board led to his demise within the confines of his prison cell. Rumours spread that Hathi Raja, in his desire to evade the watchful eyes of the medical board, employed a strategy to deceive them and secure a diagnosis. Within the confines of his cell, he chose to forsake his regular blood pressure medication and opted for an injection designed to artificially elevate his vitals. As the potion took effect, his blood pressure surged and he succumbed to a brain haemorrhage.

The situation gave rise to a lot of speculation and conjecture about the actual cause of his death. Some thought it might have been a natural occurrence, whereas others attributed it to his cunning. However, the truth remained elusive, and the real cause of his demise could never be definitively determined.

13

A Machine Errs

An error in an explosive test detection machine at Raja Bhoj Airport in Bhopal, Madhya Pradesh, triggered suspicion among security officials that a passenger was carrying drugs. When they ran the passenger's luggage through the machine, its alarm sounded, indicating the presence of narcotics in his bag.

One unusually hot summer morning, I was seated in my office when I received a call from the then SP of Bhopal, informing me about a case and detailing the actions taken by the police.

A few days later, an elderly gentleman entered my office. He seemed to be well-off but looked worried. He introduced himself as Mahesh Pratap Singh, a resident of Gwalior. He explained that he used to work as a manager at a steel plant in Bhilai until 1989, after which he moved to Gwalior, where he worked for MP Iron and Steel Company until his retirement.

'My elder son, Raj Pratap Singh, is an employee of an IT company, and my younger son Vijay Pratap Singh works for a company in Malaysia,' the gentleman said. 'Vijay completed his BE from an engineering college in Raipur in 1992. He worked for a steel company in Mumbai until 2002, after which he joined HEG at Mandideep in Bhopal. The company subsequently assigned him to Malaysia, where he currently works for Met Tube Company.'

Mahesh Pratap Singh further explained that Vijay had recently come from Malaysia to Delhi. After a few days, he went to Gwalior by the Shatabdi Express. Vijay stayed with his father for a few days before travelling to Bhopal, where he had to attend to some assignments that his company had tasked him with. After finishing his work, Vijay was scheduled to catch a flight to Delhi, from where he would return to Malaysia.

⁂

Raja Bhoj Airport in Bhopal bustled with activity as passengers of the Bhopal–Delhi flight prepared to check in. Seat number one on the flight was booked in the name of Vijay Singh. Singh arrived at the airport and entered after showing his ticket and identity card. Upon reaching the check-in counter, he placed his luggage on the X-ray machine while retaining a handbag with him. When the X-ray machine did not reveal any suspicious items, the officials issued him a boarding pass. Singh then proceeded to the security check, where he gave his handbag to the security officers for checking in the X-ray machine while getting his own security check done.

During the inspection, an SI of the security force noticed a saffron-coloured packet inside the handbag. Suspecting something amiss, he stopped the bag for physical verification. Upon requesting Singh to open the handbag, the security officials discovered several packets of spice mixture inside. When the security personnel asked Vijay Singh to open those packets, he explained that they were packets of a spice mixture of the Rawal Das brand, containing coriander powder, dry mango powder, fennel seeds and henna, which he had bought in Gwalior. Singh said that as Indian spices were not available in Malaysia, he had purchased the packets for his personal use. Despite his explanation, the security official asked a constable to put it in the explosive test detection (ETD) machine, which reported that the spices contained 4 per cent narcotics. Based on the report, the security officers and those of the airline deployed at the airport took Singh into their custody.

All of Singh's luggage, which had already been loaded on to the aircraft, was brought back, and he was asked to open those for further inspection. There were a few packets of spice mixtures in the luggage as well. Samples taken from the packets were examined using the ETD machine to see whether they contained narcotics. Singh was informed that the mango powder contained one per cent of a chemical called methyldiethanolamine (MDEA).

As this chemical falls under the scope of narcotic drugs and psychotropic substances (NDPS), the machine triggered the alarm. The shift in-charge of the security force was also informed about it. He got the packets re-examined and confirmed the presence of narcotics in the spice mixture. Subsequently, Singh was interrogated, and copies of his boarding pass and passport were obtained. The security officials then sealed the packets containing the powder and mango dust in front of Singh and took his statement. Meanwhile, a senior officer of the airline also reached the spot where the inquiry was going on. He advised the security officials to send the packets to a laboratory for further analysis rather than solely relying on the machine's reports to suspect the passenger of carrying drugs.

Mahesh informed me that the security personnel did not listen to the advice and informed the senior officers of the security force about it. Vijay Singh was escorted to the Nehru Sagar police station by a constable, accompanied by the sealed packets of the spice mixture. Representatives from the airline's security team were also sent to the Nehru Sagar police station. Upon arrival, Vijay Singh was presented before the police, and an application was submitted, detailing the incident. Immediately after that, the station in-charge informed the senior police officers about the incident. All the packets were weighed, and an FIR was registered against Vijay Singh. The police arrested Singh once the formalities were completed.

'His involvement in carrying narcotics is impossible because he is highly qualified and has a family to feed; he has been sent to jail for no fault of his. My daughter-in-law and grandchildren are alone in a foreign land, where they have nobody to help them. I am travelling between Gwalior and Bhopal almost daily to fight a legal battle against the case,' Mahesh Pratap Singh said in frustration.

The Nehru Sagar police initiated an inquiry into the case. They called the mobile forensic laboratory unit to examine the spice mixture and dry mango powder.

The laboratory technicians, however, did not find the presence of narcotics in those packets. Surprisingly, no formal report was issued by the technicians; instead, they verbally suggested that the samples be forwarded to the regional lab for further testing. Consequently, the Nehru Sagar police sent the samples to the Regional Forensic Laboratory in Bhopal for testing.

When the police did not get any reply, they sent a reminder to the laboratory after a week. There was no reply even after an additional 10 days. In a subsequent inquiry about the validity of the machine report, the officials at the laboratory returned the packets without even analysing what was inside them. They said that there was no system for MDEA checking. They also did not send the packets to any other laboratory for analysis but advised that the police send them to the Central Forensic Science Laboratory (CFSL), Hyderabad.

⟡

'I have gathered some information about the ETD machine through the internet that I want to share with you. I request you to question the officials of the security force, airline and police to uncover the truth. As the machine was made in Canada, it failed to calibrate the fragrance of Indian spices and was unsuitable to Indian conditions,' Mahesh Pratap Singh said.

According to him, the official website of the Canadian company that manufactures the machine had a video clip demonstrating how to handle it. He pointed out that the security force and airline officials were not trained in handling it, leading to errors for which his son had to bear the consequences. When I asked him about the basis of his statement, he insisted that the officials had not followed the standard procedures before operating the machine.

Vijay's father said that the airport officials had concluded that his son had carried drugs without conducting a thorough investigation. He highlighted that only standard samples of explosives were available at Bhopal airport for checking and that specimens of drugs were not available there. He questioned the ability of the ETD machine and the efficiency of the security and airline officials. Referring to the video on handling the ETD machine, he mentioned that the correct procedure involved taking a specimen and rubbing it on the surface of the luggage, wallet or handbag rather than directly dipping the swab into the real sample.

'The machine is so sensitive that it suggests the presence of drugs even if the sample of the suspected substance is in a very low quantity. If the quantity of the sample is high, the machine may give incorrect results,' Mahesh added. Additionally, as there was no chemical test kit at the airport, the results given by the ETD machine could not be re-examined.

'The ETD machine only gives reports that are examined with the help of chemical kits to confirm the correctness of the results provided by the machine, but in Vijay's case, the samples were not analysed using a chemical kit,' Mahesh pointed out.

Mahesh believed that the officials did not use their conscience. As the flight was going to Delhi, they could have sent the samples there for examination to allay their doubts. According to Vijay Singh's account to his father, the entire episode indicated that the officials of the security agency, as well as of the airline, were in a hurry to catch a drug peddler so that they might get a reward. Vijay alleged that the officials concluded that those substances contained narcotics by simply smelling and testing the mango powder and spice mixtures.

I advised Mahesh to submit an application to the Nehru Sagar police station so that the cops might look into those issues. I informed him that because the security force officials had made a case and booked his son under the NDPS Act, the police could hardly do anything about it. Everything was to be done according to the law. Mahesh Pratap Singh then submitted an application at the Nehru Sagar police station, requesting that the spice mixture and mango powder of other established brands be examined in the ETD machine at the airport so that the reports provided by it could be compared.

Upon receiving Mahesh Pratap Singh's application, the Nehru Sagar police instructed the officials of the security force and airline to examine the spice mixtures of different established brands. When the officials put spice mixtures and mango powder of other brands in the machine, the alarm sounded, indicating that there were narcotics in those items too. The concerned authorities failed to provide any manual on how to operate the machine, which indicated that the manual was not available to them. They were also unable to provide any proof that the reports provided by the machine were correct.

Meanwhile, the report from CFSL clearly stated that there was no MDEA or any other narcotic drug in the spice mixture seized from Vijay Singh. I instructed the officials to present the report before the NDPS Act court and get Vijay Singh released as quickly as possible. The police released him on a personal bond and presented the case before the special judge of the NDPS Act court, who absolved him of all charges.

I personally extended an apology to Vijay Singh and his father. The incident had caused Vijay undue stress and had an adverse effect on his job in Malaysia. This case highlighted the misuse of the ETD machine, which appeared to be calibrated solely for detecting narcotics and explosives. Maybe that was why it had set off a false alarm as soon as the spice mixture powder and mango powder were tested. It was evident that the machine required adjustments to function effectively in Indian conditions. Otherwise, it would continue to ruin the lives of many innocent people. The incident still saddens me—an innocent person had to suffer without any fault. I was determined to get Vijay Singh released and restore his tarnished image through media intervention.

In addition to urging the media to emphasize the case's resolution, I tried to save Vijay's job. The incident left me disheartened because the system has ruined the careers and families of many innocent people. Despite Vijay Singh's pleas of innocence and requests for a re-examination of the suspicious spice mixture, he was disregarded, harassed and unjustly incarcerated for 57 days.

The incident that occurred because of the errors of some officials tarnished the security force's image, which is one of the country's premier security agencies.

This sorrowful episode remains etched in my memory even today.

14

Freed from the Kidnappers

A prominent businessman and his family found themselves in a nerve-racking ordeal when one of their own was kidnapped. The captors demanded a substantial ransom, setting off a high-stakes race against time.

On a chilly winter morning, I received a call from Anil Sharma, the in-charge of the Narsinghgarh police station. He informed me that a missing person's case had been lodged for Manoj Patidar, who operated a stone crusher in Mehboob Ganj. It appeared that Patidar, a resident of Narsinghgarh, had vanished mysteriously, leaving his car abandoned near a roadside food outlet.

When Sharma had gone to Mehboob Ganj to probe the incident, Patidar's employees told him that two individuals in a white car had come to the worksite to visit Patidar two days before his disappearance. The workers also said that Patidar had gone to have a cup of tea with those people and had been untraceable since then. The employees had not been able to see the faces of those individuals as they had stood far away from the factory site.

The owner of the roadside food outlet, near which Patidar's car had been found, informed Anil Sharma that Patidar had visited his outlet two days ago with two individuals. As Patidar's companions stood a few yards away from the outlet, neither the owner nor the workers of the food joint had been able to see their faces, partly because of the darkness and partly because of the distance. They could only identify the companions to be men. Having been briefed by Sharma, I immediately decided to visit the scene of the incident and speak with Manoj's family members, informing both the SP in Bhopal and the police station in-charge of Mehboob Ganj of my intentions.

I instructed Salil Sharma, the cyber cell in-charge, to obtain Manoj Patidar's call details and locations. Accompanied by the in-charge of Mehboob Ganj police station, Ajay Nair, I made my way to the spot from where Patidar had gone missing. Despite engaging in discussions with the employees of the food outlet and the stone-crushing factory, we failed to gather any substantial information that would aid in the investigation. Subsequently, I requested the presence of Patidar's family at the scene. Jitendra, Patidar's brother, arrived and revealed that Manoj had been missing from home for the last two days and his mobile phone was unreachable. I told Jitendra, 'As soon as you get any news about Manoj, you should contact the police.'

By the time we returned to Bhopal, Salil Sharma had extracted Manoj's call details and locations, which we sifted through but failed to draw any conclusion. We decided to continue our work and discussed the case with the DIG in Bhopal and the SPs in Bhopal and Rajgarh.

It was 9 p.m., and as I was about to leave my office, I received a call from Anil Sharma. He said that someone had contacted Jitendra using Manoj's phone, demanding him to pay a ransom of ₹20 lakh if he didn't wish to find Manoj's body in pieces. I immediately consulted DIG Ashok Awasthi. It was not hard to conclude that a few goons had abducted Manoj for ransom. After discussing the situation with senior officers of the Bhopal Zone, it was decided to keep the incident away from the eyes of the media. We feared that Manoj would lose his life if the media brought attention to the case. Therefore, we did not register a case of kidnapping for ransom but left the FIR column and diary blank to fill afterwards.

The decision taken was not in line with legal protocols, but our aim was to save the life of the kidnapped and collar the culprits. Hence, we prioritized humanity over law in this case. We informed the senior officers in police headquarters about our decision and received their support. They advised us to apprehend the criminals as quickly as possible.

The following day, we visited Manoj's family in plain clothes.

We asked his family members whether they suspected anyone, but their reply was negative. I told them that the police were very cautious about not releasing the case information to the media because that would only alert the kidnappers and endanger Manoj's life. We also advised them to tell outsiders that Manoj was out of station and would soon return and that if anyone wanted to know about us, to tell them that the TI was known to the family, so he visited the house to have a cup of tea. We further told the family members that till we caught the culprits and rescued Manoj from their clutches, we would not visit them; if we had any questions, we would call them to meet us at some location.

❧

Back in Bhopal, I set up a small team consisting of the DIG, the TIs of Mehboob Ganj and Narsinghgarh, SI Jeetendra Pathak, Salil Sharma and me.

I spoke to the SPs of Bhopal and Rajgarh and discussed the developments in detail. The police station in-charges of both places were instructed to regularly inform the senior officers about developments in the case. To prevent media attention, we kept certain senior officers away from the overt inquiry, opting for covert operations using private vehicles and plain clothes officers. Through the cyber cell, we tracked the location of the call made to Jitendra using Manoj's phone. The call details did not mention any area beyond Hamidia Road, so we waited for the next call. The culprits called Jitendra again after a day's gap, saying that he should come to Betul Highway between Mandideep and Obaidullaganj with ₹20 lakh to secure his brother's release. They also warned Jitendra against informing the police. Jitendra followed our advice and told the culprits that he had informed neither the police nor the media about it. Jitendra informed Anil Sharma who, in turn, called me. I advised Anil Sharma to suggest Jitendra to leave his home with a suitcase and proceed to Bhopal in a hired vehicle. I also advised Sharma to use a private vehicle for himself and that I would follow them in another private car along with the DIG and the SI of the cyber cell.

Though in different cars, we maintained communication with one another. On reaching Mandideep, we stopped our car a few metres from Jitendra's destination and waited there for the criminals. We waited for more than half an hour, but there was no communication from the kidnappers. We decided to return to Bhopal. Just as we neared Baloda, I received a call from the cyber cell that Manoj's mobile showed his location to be on the Badi–Bareli road near the Jabalpur highway. To stay updated on Manoj's location, I instructed the mobile company to send regular service messages to his phone, as the kidnappers were using Manoj's mobile phone only to communicate with his brother. Otherwise, Manoj's mobile phone remained inactive most of the time.

We headed back towards Badi. As we reached Obaidullaganj, Jitendra received a call from the kidnappers saying that they were waiting for him there, but as he did not go to the spot, the kidnappers had arrived at Badi. He was with us instead as part of our strategy. We refrained from directing him towards a less-travelled road to avoid drawing attention to our surveillance, which could have aroused suspicions among the kidnappers.

Jitendra was then asked by the kidnapper to come to Badi and hand over the ransom. As per my advice, Jitendra told the criminals to let his brother talk to him, but the kidnappers only asked him to reach the spot with the money without trying to be smart. I instructed Jitendra to tell the criminals that because it was night and the road was empty, he was returning to Bhopal. Although the kidnappers warned of dire consequences, we chose to regroup in Bhopal for the night. The following morning, Jitendra received another call instructing him to keep the ransom ready and that he would be provided further details about the delivery location.

At that time, Manoj's mobile location indicated that he was near Sudarshan Hotel, adjacent to Hamidia Road.

Sensing a potential breakthrough, we decided to position ourselves inside Sudarshan Hotel with the ransom money. Being acquainted with the hotel owner, I sought his cooperation for our operation. My team and I came up with a strategic plan and deployed three police officers in the guise of waiters. I disguised myself as a villager, wearing a gamchha around my neck, sitting in a corner of the hotel with Anil Sharma. Meanwhile, I instructed the SI of the cyber cell to take charge of the billing counter.

We waited at the hotel for several hours, yet no communication came from the kidnappers. Eventually, we decided to return to the office but kept our team ready in case of any developments. Jitendra received a call at 7 p.m. from the kidnappers, inquiring about the ransom. Jitendra informed them that he had waited for them at Sudarshan Hotel for several hours, but had returned home when they failed to show up. The caller told him to go back to Sudarshan Hotel. We immediately rushed back to the hotel.

The cyber cell informed us that Manoj's phone indicated the location of the kidnappers to be New Market, the main shopping centre in Bhopal. Another call from the kidnapper instructed Jitendra to come to New Market. We immediately left Sudarshan Hotel in separate cars and followed the vehicle carrying Jitendra and Anil Sharma, maintaining a certain distance from them. Though we kept our distance from one another, we communicated with each other over the phone to get updates.

When we reached New Market, the kidnappers' location was near the Maulana Azad National School of Design in Vaishali Nagar. Upon further instructions from the kidnappers for Jitendra to move to Kerwa Dam Road with the money, we promptly reached there. However, upon our arrival, the caller redirected Jitendra to Ramnagar Road, so we changed our location once again. The kidnappers' whereabouts were then pinpointed to Bhadbhada Road, near a food joint close to a burial ground. Jitendra had hardly reached Ramnagar Road when the kidnappers told him to move towards Ramnagar Dam, an isolated area surrounded by forests and hillocks. This cat-and-mouse chase continued for many hours, and we were oblivious to when night fell; we realized it was late in the day only when we looked at the empty road through the windows of our cars. Aware of the potential risk of being seen by the culprits who could be hiding in the woods under the cover of the night, we decided to retreat.

When we returned to Bhopal, the kidnappers asked Jitendra about his failure to reach the Ramnagar Dam where they had been waiting for him. Jitendra gave them a rehearsed explanation, citing fear of the darkness as his reason for not complying with their demand. He proposed meeting during daylight hours to complete the exchange.

The next day too, the kidnappers played hide-and-seek with Jitendra. They continued to demand ransom, arranging rendezvous points, but when Jitendra would ask them to come to a certain place, they would not agree with him. This was a strategic move aimed at shifting the kidnapper's operational advantage to our favourable terrain, ensuring that we had the upper hand in apprehending them. Our team thus responded to calls directing us to various locations including Badi, Dehgaon, Bamhori, Udaipura, Sultanpur, Gyarah Mile, Baloda, Habibganj station, Roshanpura, Jawahar Chowk, a bus stand, Kotra and Ten Number stop. Despite our efforts to cordon off these areas, the kidnappers managed to elude us each time.

It seemed that the kidnappers were keeping an eye on the places where they called Jitendra but they could not muster up enough courage to take the ransom. Their continual relocation made it challenging for us to gather intelligence as they utilized Manoj's mobile phone. I then instructed the mobile phone company to suspend outgoing calls from Manoj's phone. The next day, there was a call on Manoj's landline number at his house. This prompted a warning from the kidnappers when they attempted to make contact via the Patidars' landline, who told the kidnappers that they hadn't done anything.

The Patidars were right; neither Jitendra nor his family members were informed about the fact that the outgoing calls from Manoj's phone had been stopped.

The cyber cell traced the call back to a PCO in Roshanpura. We had already implemented caller identification on the Patidars' landline number. Whenever Manoj's family received any call, we would get the number from the cyber cell.

The kidnappers called from different PCOs in Bhopal to make ransom demands. When we contacted the PCO operators, they said that two individuals on a motorcycle had visited their call centres; they would swiftly enter, make the call and leave, speaking in hushed tones so that no one was able to overhear. The person making the call was described as a fair man with curly hair, wearing black trousers and a yellow T-shirt. I directed the PCO operators to notify us immediately in case the kidnappers returned.

The three kidnappers turned out to be very clever, leading us on a wild goose chase across multiple locations and PCOs for several days. The kidnappers asked Jitendra to walk from Habibganj railway station to the Board Office Square with the bag containing the ransom, but the police also spread their snare everywhere in the city so that the criminals would fall into it.

As instructed, Jitendra took a stroll, with us trailing behind him cautiously. When we neared a petrol pump in the area, Salil Sharma and I spotted someone who seemed like our suspect. We jumped out from our vehicle and collared him. Just as we caught hold of the rogue, many people began to crowd around us, prompting us to identify ourselves and explain the situation.

The suspect was taken to the control room, where the police grilled him and he confessed to his crimes. He revealed that Manoj was being held captive in a rented room near the police headquarters in Jahangirabad. The accused also said, 'My associate is keeping an eye on Patidar. He is carrying a pistol to scare him.'

On learning that we arrested one of the kidnappers near the petrol pump, his associates ran to the rented house where Patidar was being held and informed his accomplice to escape from that place, leaving their hostage behind because the police were chasing them. But before they could free Manoj and escape, the police seized them and rescued Manoj from their clutches.

SP Jaydeep Prasad chose to confront the criminal alone to prevent any reckless action on the part of the kidnappers, which might harm passers-by. In a flash, he pounced upon the crook, who tried to wriggle out of the officer's grip but could not do so.

The mastermind behind Manoj Patidar's kidnapping was identified as Naveen Rathore. He was so smart that he had kept Patidar in a house near the police headquarters to avoid suspicion. Upon his arrest, a pistol and live cartridges were seized from him. Further interrogation led to the apprehension of another criminal from the Noor Bagh area in the city. During interrogation, Rathore confessed to resorting to kidnapping due to mounting debts, intending to repay them using the ransom from the Patidar family.

Rathore's father was a constable in the police department, so he was acquainted with the functioning of the Special Task Force. He also knew that phone companies could provide information about the kidnapper's locations. That was why he kept changing the location of the ransom drop.

Originally from Bhind, Rathore worked as a contractor in Bhopal and went to Manoj to buy building materials. Upon learning of the Patidar family's wealth, Rathore hatched a plan to kidnap Manoj. However, due to police intervention, he was unable to extort even a single penny from the family.

Recognizing the dangers associated with paying ransom to kidnappers, we had advised the Patidars against compliance from the outset of the investigation. This precaution was taken to prevent the possibility of the criminals taking the money and then harming the hostage to evade capture by law enforcement.

Epilogue

I was destined to be a cop. Despite initially opting for the Indian Forest Service over the IPS, I later reconsidered, believing that the latter would be a better fit for me. However, by the time I made this decision, six months had already elapsed since I had declined the IPS offer. Disheartened, I sought solace at the Sankat Mochan Temple in Varanasi, where I fervently prayed to Lord Hanuman for a miracle, hoping for another chance.

Upon returning to my hostel room after my prayers, I was pleasantly surprised as soon as I opened the door. There, lying on the floor of my room was the long-awaited letter from the Ministry of Home Affairs, Government of India, offering me a final opportunity to join the IPS. My fervent wish had been granted, and I eagerly accepted the offer, embarking on my journey in the police department.

I joined the Sardar Vallabhbhai Patel National Police Academy as an officer of the IPS. During one of my initial conversations with Mr Aftab Ahmad Ali, the then director of the Academy, I shared with him my academic achievements—including a PhD in Forest Ecology and published research papers—as well as my experiences in the Indian Forest Service. His candid remarks resonated deeply with me, 'Gentleman, you are in the wrong service. It seems that you crave praise. In the police service, you should not expect accolades. Be ready to endure criticism. You are lucky if you receive some praise.'

As an IPS officer of the Madhya Pradesh cadre, I embarked on field training in Ratlam under the guidance of SP S.K. Rout. Immersed in my duties, I learned to downplay my achievements and thoroughly engage in the art of policing. Once when I was on night patrol, I encountered a constable neglecting his duty.

Acting on my commitment to uphold the integrity of the police force, I reported the incident to SP Rout, seeking action against the constable. However, the situation took an unexpected turn when the constable lodged a complaint against me, falsely accusing me of misconduct. I was shocked! I prided myself on being temperate and someone who never used foul language. However, this marked the first complaint against me in my career as a police officer.

I turned to SP Rout for guidance, whose words of wisdom stayed with me, 'In the police department, there will always be complaints against you for things you haven't done. If you had been drunk or beaten up the constable, nothing would have happened. He is the first madcap you have encountered, and there are many such people in the department. Just forget it, and be cheerful.' He further advised me to take up some hobbies so that whenever I faced a rough patch in my career, I could cope with it with a smiling face.

A few days after the incident, the DIG of Ujjain Range, H.P. Singh, came for an inspection, and I spent three days with him. He advised me to let go of my regular lifestyle, stating that enjoying life's simple pleasures is not possible in the police department. He further added, 'Eat food whenever you get it, and rest whenever you have time. Get enough sleep.'

Those who choose the khaki uniform cannot avoid pressure. The mental and physical strains they endure from dawn till dusk naturally drain their energy. Police officers are surrounded by criminals whose weapons are always ready to harm them. Nevertheless, these officers rarely receive appreciation, which sometimes disappoints them.

We deal with diverse individuals, so their responses are unpredictable. Expectations from us are high, and we cannot always meet them. I would say that police officers frequently encounter failure in one way or another. Quick success is a bonus that we seldom receive. Handling failures is challenging because people often play the blame game and shift responsibilities to one another, which further complicates the problem. I always suggested to my colleagues to learn to live with failures and criticism and be prepared for infamy. These are professional hazards.

In *John North Willys*, Elbert Hubbard writes, 'Do nothing, say nothing and be nothing, and you'll never be criticized.' That just doesn't sound like much of a life, does it? Therefore, it is necessary to learn to accept or ignore criticism.

If you have not learnt how to do so, you will spend the rest of your life avoiding doing or saying anything that might attract criticism, like a ship constantly veering away from every gust of wind. Will you ever reach your destination like that?

The wisdom I received at the outset of my career remained a guiding light, bolstering my determination as I faced challenges head-on.

Reflecting on my extensive journey as an IPS officer of more than 34 years, I find myself pondering over two fundamental questions: What have I gained from my service; and what have I given back to society in exchange for the privileges and respect bestowed upon me? Throughout my career, my profession has instilled in me values of punctuality, discipline, a strong work ethic, empathy and compassion, embodying the traits of a dedicated police officer.

In *Shackle the Storm*, I have endeavoured to encapsulate this essence. Amidst the challenges, maintaining composure and upholding the truth remains paramount. Despite the tumultuous nature of the work, it is imperative for a police officer to remain steadfast, especially in the face of adversity. Through dedication and unwavering commitment, I have strived to contribute positively to society, ensuring justice and safety for all. The journey has been one of learning, growth and service to the community.

Acknowledgements

My mother's teachings and my father's guidance have been the guiding stars that have illuminated my path throughout my professional and personal journey.

My mother has been my best teacher.

She was a devotee of Lord Rama and read the *Ramcharitmanas* daily. She often said, 'Lord Rama endured all the sufferings of life. He renounced his kingdom and lived as a hermit. Life is full of suffering; one must confront it with a smile.' Through the *Ramcharitmanas*, she taught me how to stay calm and humble in every situation.

She often said, 'You're not wealthy, and you don't belong to any specific religion or caste. You are a human being with assigned tasks that you must fulfil with humility, as your circumstances could have been different. Avoid boasting, and be prepared to handle criticism.'

Although it has been long since my mother departed for the eternal world, her teachings continue to shine before me like the Pole Star on the horizon. They will remain with me until I close my eyes.

To my wife, Kalpana, and my beloved daughters, Aishwarya and Arunima, I express my heartfelt gratitude for their unwavering support and understanding. They have been the pillars of strength in my life, providing me with balance and warmth during challenging times.

I am further privileged to be supported by remarkable individuals whose contributions have been invaluable in writing this book. My heartfelt gratitude goes to esteemed senior journalist Rasheed Kidwai; talented author, columnist and my literary consultant Atul K. Thakur; and the incredible team at Rupa Publications.

Dr Abdul Tahir and Farhan Ansari's constant encouragement has played a crucial role in inspiring me to pen this book. I am deeply indebted to Pushpendra Mishra and Arup Chakraborty for their resolute feedback and steadfast support throughout this journey.

Special acknowledgement goes to my fellow police officers, whose names have been mentioned in the preceding chapters, for being an integral part of the extraordinary journey embodied in *Shackle the Storm*.

Finally, I extend my heartfelt thanks to all the readers who have embraced my book. Your appreciation and encouragement fuel my passion for storytelling.